MW01517815

MEINRAD SCHÜTTER
MAVERICK SWISS COMPOSER

MEINRAD SCHÜTTER
MAVERICK SWISS COMPOSER

UTE STOECKLIN

Translated by
CHRIS WALTON

TOCCATA
CLASSICS

First published by Toccata Press, 2024
© Ute Stoecklin, 2024

British Library Cataloguing in Publication Data
A catalogue record for this book is available from the British Library.

ISBN 978-0-907689-70-6

This is a revised version of Ute Stoecklin's *Meinrad Schütter 1910–2006. Lebenswerk Musik oder 'Die Kunst, sich nicht stören zu lassen'*, published in 2010 by Musikverlag Müller & Schade AG in Bern.

Set in 11 on 12 point Minion Pro
by ALN Design, St Albans

Contents

		Page
Foreword		9
Acknowledgements		10
The Author		11
The Translator		11
1	A Composer of the Alpine Region	13
2	Parents, Families and Home	17
3	Childhood and Early Youth	23
4	Friends of Youth	34
5	The 1930s: Early Works	41
6	Rome, 1939	54
7	Military Service, *Medea* and Marriage	59
8	Studies with Paul Hindemith, 1951–54	67
9	In the Zurich Opera	76
10	Friends and Colleagues	84
11	The Piano Concerto	94
12	Vagabond Poet: The Later Years	106
13	Chamber Music in Vilnius	114
14	A New Century and a Symphony	119
Afterword		
Meinrad Schütter: The Music and the Man	*Chris Walton*	129
Catalogue of Works		
Operas		137
Ballets		138
Orchestral Works		139
Concertos		140
Chamber Music and Works for Solo Strings or Winds		141
Organ Works		147
Piano Duets and Duos		148
Piano Solo		148
Choral Works with Accompaniment		152
Choral Works *a cappella*		153
Songs for Voice(s) and Ensemble or Orchestra		157

Works for Speaker with Accompaniment   160
Songs for Voice and Organ   160
Songs for Voice and Piano   162

Discography   169
Select Bibliography   172

Index of Schütter's Works   175
General Index   179

List of Illustrations

Meinrad Schütter in Basel, 1994   12
Map of Graubünden from the 1620s   14
Chur around 1900   15
Meinrad Schütter's parents, Joseph and Emilie Schütter   18
The Obertor and Ochsenplatz in Chur, c. 1900   19
Joseph Schütter, c. 1930   20
Schütter's 'wrong' grandmother Sophie Hegner, c. 1895   24
Chur and its environs, in a late-nineteenth-century map   24
'Klein-Waldegg', built by Meinrad Schütter's grandmother in 1899   25
Meinrad Schütter with his parents, brother Pepi and grandparents   26
Pepi and Meinrad Schütter, c. 1913   27
Klein-Waldegg with its German internee soldiers
    during the First World War   28
Pepi and Meinrad Schütter in Arosa, 1924   29
Joseph Schütter on the path to Meinrad Schütter's school, c. 1920   31
The first-ever car trip, to Davos,
    for local dignitaries of Chur, c. 1923   32
Emanuel Bernard and Meinrad Schütter, 1981   35
Meinrad Schütter at the organ, c. 1928   36
Nandor Währing and Meinrad Schütter, c. 1929   37
Nandor Währing's pass for his failed emigration to Paraguay, 1948   39
The Zurich Conservatoire, c. 1930   42
Carl Vogler's letter to Meinrad Schütter of 30 January 1940   43
Claudia Mengelt (later Claudia Schütter) in Splügen
    in the mid-1930s   50
Meinrad Schütter in Rome, 1939   55
Guido Gonzato and family with Schütter, c. 1946   57
Guido Gonzato, *Sera*: oil and tempera on board, 1943   58
Schütter in the Swiss Army, Sargans, c. 1940   60
Schütter in the Swiss Army, San Bernardino, 1942   62
The Zurich Opera House in 1952, with the prompter's box
    in the middle of the stage   65
Paul Hindemith with his class at Zurich University, c. 1954   68
A performance of *Dr Joggeli sött go Birli schüttle* in Basel,
    25 January 2009   73

Schütter in 1955   74
Rehearsals in Zurich for Rolf Liebermann's *Penelope* in 1954   77
Franz Rederer: portrait of Meinrad Schütter,
    dated 16 March 1956   78
Claudia and Meinrad Schütter, New Year's Eve, 1961   80
Claudia Schütter in the prompter's box
    in the Zurich Opera House, c. 1970   81
Küsnacht, as seen from Lake Zurich in 2012   81
Schütter in the 1960s   82
Father Karl Weber and Schütter in 2000   83
The Conti Restaurant behind the Zurich Opera House, 1972   85
Walter Mehring in the Hotel Opera in Zurich, 1976   86
The painter Adolf Herbst in 1975   87
Philipp and Verena Zinsli, c. 1990   89
Verena Zinsli: Meinrad Schütter at the piano, c. 1990   91
Schütter at his desk in Küsnacht in 1989   102
Verena Zinsli: Meinrad Schütter in 1990   104
Schütter in 1998   107
Flandrina von Salis and Schütter at a song recital
    chez Zinsli, 1993   112
Ute Stoecklin, Schütter and Stefania Huonder at a song
    recital in Ratzeburg, 1997   115
Schütter at the organ in Zollikon in May 2002   120
The birthday concert in Küsnacht in 2000   123
After a Liederabend in Basel: Schütter, Ute Stoecklin,
    Andrea Scartazzini and Michael Leibundgut   124
Ludwig Stocker, Ute Stoecklin and Schütter in Stocker's
    studio in Basel, 2003   125
Schütter in his last years   127

Foreword

Meinrad Schütter (1910–2006) was one of many musical personalities who found themselves pushed to the margins of the cultural scene in a century marked by multiple wars and social upheaval. Hardly any of the significant Swiss composers born before the First World War were able to sustain their reputation beyond the Second. Othmar Schoeck (1886–1957) and Erich Schmid (1907–2000), for example, were forgotten for much of the latter half of the twentieth century. Only those Swiss composers who emigrated – first and foremost Arthur Honegger (1892–1955) and Frank Martin (1890–1974) – were able to evade such oblivion.

The fate of Schoeck, Schmid and all was shared by Meinrad Schütter, who had only just begun to enjoy his first composing successes in 1939 when war broke out, ushering in a period of isolation for Switzerland that largely cut off its composers from the broader European scene. Schütter's case was perhaps different in that his was a decidedly introverted personality that was averse to any active attempts to secure public recognition. But he took pleasure in observing things from the periphery, and as a politically minded man he developed a keen interest in the events and trends in the world in general and in the arts in particular, always remaining alert to what he saw and heard. In his later years, he more or less belonged to the townscape of Küsnacht – standing in his hat and coat, carrying a newspaper and a pocket score, with a smouldering cigarette between his fingers. One often saw him thus at railway stations, bus stops or in the queue at a concert hall: constantly on the move, with the insatiable curiosity of an artistic spirit and an unquenchable appetite to learn new things.

This book is a revised version of my German-language biography of Meinrad Schütter, published by Müller & Schade in Bern on the occasion of the composer's centenary in 2010. I was friends with Schütter for over three decades, and in the latter half of our friendship I also edited and performed many of his works. Schütter later expressed a wish that I should one day write about his life, and so I began keeping a record of our conversations. In the text which follows, I have not footnoted the source every time I quote from what he told me. Writing about him has been a journey of discovery that often brought about a shift in my own perspective of his biography and *œuvre*. I have here endeavoured to portray the man and the composer in the context of his time, while also incorporating many of his own colourful but often fragmentary reminiscences. His posthumous letters and papers, held today by the Chur City Archives, further helped me to fill out my narrative.

To judge from reviews of his recordings over the past 30 years, the Anglo-Saxon world seems especially receptive to Schütter's music. Thus I hope that presenting this appraisal of the life and works of this unusual, quiet man in an English-language book might prove to be the right step at the right time and will help to promote an awareness and understanding of his music.

Acknowledgements

I am grateful to the Stadtarchiv Chur and the Zentralbibliothek Zürich for providing access to their holdings. The City of Chur has kindly provided financial assistance for the publication of this book, as have the Stiftung Lienhard-Hunger and the Boner Stiftung für Kunst und Kultur, both in Chur. I am further indebted to the Meinrad Schütter-Gesellschaft for its support. The images in this book have all been provided by the Meinrad Schütter-Gesellschaft with the following exceptions: the photo of the Zurich Conservatoire is held by the Baugeschichtliches Archiv Zürich (Creative Commons), those of Claudia Schütter in the 1930s and of *Die Fledermaus* in Zurich by the Stadtarchiv Chur (shelfmarks N 168.0511 and N 168.0709), those of the Zurich Opera House in 1952, of Adolf Herbst and of Walter Mehring by the ETH Bibliothek Zürich, Bildarchiv (Comet Photo AG, Zürich/Com_M01-0145-0005, Vogt, Jules/Com_L24-0060-0001-0002 and Schmid, Walter/Com_L25-0168-0001-0002 respectively); the photo of the Conti Restaurant is held by the Baugeschichtliches Archiv der Stadt Zürich (BAZ_125798).

It only remains for me to thank all the friends whose support and advice have made this book possible.

Ute Stoecklin
Binningen, 2023

The Author

Ute Stoecklin is a musician, gallerist and curator, and an author on music and cultural topics. As a pianist, she has performed the music of contemporary composers extensively in Switzerland and abroad, on the radio and on commercial recordings. She has also moderated concerts and interdisciplinary events.

Over many years, she invested her energies in performing and promoting the music of the Swiss composer Meinrad Schütter (1910–2006). She compiled the first catalogue of his works in 1993–94, updating it thereafter on a regular basis, and in 1990 began publishing his songs and chamber works with Nepomuk Verlag in Aarau and Basel (which has since been taken over by Breitkopf & Härtel). She is a founding member of the Meinrad Schütter Society and its current chairwoman. She has run the Concert Gallery Maison 44 in Basel since 2002, for which she developed an interdisciplinary concept with programmes combining contemporary art, music, literature and science.

The Translator

Chris Walton studied at the universities of Cambridge, Oxford, Zurich and Munich. He was head of the Music Department of the Zentralbibliothek Zürich for ten years before being appointed chair of music at the University of Pretoria. He moved back to Switzerland in 2008 and lives today in Solothurn. He is an Honorary Professor at Africa Open Institute (Stellenbosch University) and runs two research projects at the Bern Academy of the Arts for the Swiss National Science Foundation. He has published widely on Austro-German and Swiss music.

Meinrad Schütter in Basel, 1994

1
A Composer of the Alpine Region

And as I walked through the sublime, empty regions of the high Alps, among clouds, flowery meadows and cliffs above the realms of men: the dwarflike splendour of palaces, the florid pomp of priestly temples, the paltry grandeur of nations faded from my mind – those ephemeral dustmites of the globe. It seemed to me as if I could hear God Himself speaking from the majesty of his marvellous kingdom.

Heinrich Zschokke[1]

Free in the solitude of the forests, far from the city, I looked down on it with distaste. Was this perhaps already my aversion to civilisation, which was so ugly, while the forest and the deer remained to me so primordially paradisiacal?

Meinrad Schütter[2]

The German writer Heinrich Zschokke (1771–1848) lived during the dawn of the Romantic era, when the mountainous landscapes of Switzerland began to attract poets, painters and adventurers from all over Europe. They hiked across the country, painting it and praising it in poetry and song, idealising this alpine world with its unspoilt nature as a counterpart to the supposed unnaturalness of civilisation. Jean-Jacques Rousseau saw it thus, as did Schiller somewhat later in his *Wilhelm Tell*, where the Swiss Alps came to signify individual freedom.

Graubünden (also known as the 'Grisons'), the home canton of the composer Meinrad Schütter, is the largest Swiss canton and almost entirely alpine in its geography. It boasts some 153 valleys, and while there are indeed passes and old mule tracks that over the centuries remained always open to trade and traffic, the onset of winter used to cut off most of the smaller valleys from the outside world for many months at a time. There were downsides to these circumstances – not least excessive consumption of alcohol and a degree of inbreeding – but the populations of the isolated village communities hidden deep in the valleys or high on the mountains also brought forth extraordinary, original personalities commensurate with their environment, their landscapes and nature. In the old democratic

---

[1] Heinrich Zschokke, *Eine Selbstschau*, Sauerländer, Aarau, 1842, p. 65.
[2] Notes on his childhood (c. 1980), manuscript held today in the Schütter archive in the Chur City Archives.

Map of Graubünden from the 1620s,
showing the extent to which the canton is riven by valleys

order of Switzerland, its citizens did not have to obey any overarching authority. And these alpine landscapes offered opportunities for lateral thinkers and individualists to thrive.

Schütter was always fascinated by both the structure of the alpine landscapes around him and by their ancient history, for these age-old mountains seemed to him to touch the eternal. Once, on a mountain hike with me in the Schanfigg Valley between Chur and Arosa, he said:

> The Alps of Graubünden seem sad to me and make me feel melancholic when compared to the Alps of Canton Valais. These here are older, and the mountains have been worn away earlier. I feel this as if I could read them, like they were a poetic motif. Graubünden is older, more venerable, and will die sooner. These mountains are 'old ladies' […]. It's like the poet Gottfried Keller says: the star he can see in the sky has long since been extinguished, but its light is still travelling to us […]. Look: what I see here has already gone. This world makes me melancholic.[3]

These mighty landscapes with their storms, mists, clouds, atmospheric refractions of light and sensory illusions are rich in legends, fairy tales and myths. Their interweaving of time, history, nature, literature and music

---

[3] Schütter in conversation, 13 May 1994.

Chur around 1900

intrigued Schütter from an early age. As he grew up in a strictly Catholic home, the stories of his childhood featured first and foremost the legends of the saints – these were the first heroes to inspire his imagination – but also of his immediate surroundings and an untamed nature animated by spirits of the forest and field, such as the Scaläratobel ravine just outside Chur, where the locals claimed evil things lurked at night. And Schütter, too, was an inveterate storyteller. He told stories all the time – sometimes short tales, sometimes very short, and sometimes far too long (as even his good friends sometimes complained). They were stories both true and untrue, and stories that were both (which is often what makes a good story in the first place; his were sometimes very good indeed).

The origins of Graubünden lie in the 'Grey Confederations', a kind of parallel Switzerland that had emerged during the Thirty Years' War under the leadership of Jürg Jenatsch (1596–1639), a Protestant priest and soldier who converted to Catholicism. The diversity of this mountain canton also extends to the languages that are spoken there, with their abundant tonal colours and dialects. Some 2,000 years ago, after the Romans conquered the Alpine region, their vernacular was combined with the local Celtic tongue to form a peculiar form of Vulgar Latin that then evolved into (Rhaeto) Rumansh,[4] a language that has survived in Graubünden to the present day, is spoken by some 40,000 of its inhabitants, and was designated the fourth national language of Switzerland in 1936. It always held a special

---

[4] Linus Brunner and Alfred Toth, *Die rätische Sprache – enträtselt*, Amt für Kulturpflege des Kantons St Gallen, St Gallen, 1987.

fascination for Meinrad Schütter because of its innate musicality in the shaping of its vowels and the pungency of its consonants, and his output includes numerous settings of Rumansh texts – individual songs, choral works and even a song-cycle.

Industrialisation in the nineteenth century brought to Graubünden many heroic feats of engineering in tunnel and railway construction, though the onset of early capitalism in Switzerland was viewed with no little concern by figures such as the Zurich writer Gottfried Keller (1819–90), whose brittle, occasionally patriotic poetry was close to Meinrad Schütter's heart. Although he set Keller's words to music only once,[5] Schütter took particular delight in the tales of Keller's drunken nights with his friends in the 'Öpfelchammer' pub (literally the 'apple chamber') in the old town of Zurich, which still exists; Schütter himself enjoyed its convivial atmosphere to the full on his not infrequent evenings there.

Schütter was deeply influenced by all the different cultures of his native canton of Graubünden – the German, the Rhaeto-Romanic and the Italian. It was as if he had absorbed the timbres, lines and rhythms of the mountain landscapes of his childhood and of the rugged peaks of the Montalin and Calanda. He was able to bear witness to almost an entire century, and in the final year of his life, shortly before his 95th birthday, he remarked that he sometimes felt as if he were able to gaze over the whole of Switzerland as with the eyes of an eagle.

---

[5] In his *Morgen*, for male-voice choir and piano (1986).

2
Parents, Families and Home

Meinrad Schütter was born in the early morning of 21 September 1910 on the second floor of the house at Grabenstrasse 7 in Chur, opposite the municipal theatre. That same day, a fire broke out in the yard of a nearby gas factory, triggering fears of a major explosion. Half the city was soon up and about. As a member of the volunteer fire brigade, even the new father, Joseph Johann Schütter, had to take part in the fire-fighting efforts of the citizenry. A major catastrophe was averted, though Schütter later took delight in a self-ironic insistence on the symbolism of Chur's conflagration coinciding with the nearby birth of a composer.

The cellar of the Schütters' house was the site of the soap manufactory belonging to the Hegner family on Schütter's mother's side. Their matriarch was Sophie Hegner, *née* Gut, who went down in the family annals as the composer's 'wrong' grandmother after their actual familial relationships – concealed at the time on account of reigning social conventions – were revealed many years later.[1] The origins of Schütter's family lie on the major north-south axis that leads from Germany in the north to Italy in the south, taking in the Rhine Valley upriver from Lake Constance to the Rumansh-speaking highlands of Canton Graubünden.

Graubünden itself begins a little to the west of the old, tiny city of Sargans. This region, the so-called 'Bündner Herrschaft', is a broad valley full of vineyards, castles and chateaux, and at the foot of a wooded ridge one finds the little village of Vilters, nestled alongside the larger village of Wangs (the two villages have long since become a single municipal unit). The Schütter family is said to have been resident in Vilters for a long time – too long to be able to trace when they first arrived there. No one bearing that surname lives there today, but until recently there were still some who recalled a time when the Schütters were common thereabouts.

Schütter's great-grandfather was a dyer; he was poor, and had many children. One of these children – Schütter's grandfather – was apparently highly musical and played several instruments, though his desire to become a teacher was thwarted when his father died, and the guardian appointed to him squandered what little money was left. He therefore

---

[1] Discussed on pp. 21–22, below.

Meinrad Schütter's parents, Joseph and Emilie Schütter

did an apprenticeship as a painter instead. Schütter later recalled this grandfather as a man with kind, gentle eyes; quiet, sad and contemplative.[2] He fell on hard times at an early age, and moved to St Gallen before finally arriving in Chur with his large family in around 1894–95, where he set up a painting business.

Schütter's father, Joseph Johann (1876–1935), was eighteen years old at the time of the move and attending secondary school in Sargans; he then joined his father in the family business in Chur. He developed an interest in politics early on, sat on various committees and later became president of the local trade association and Mayor of Chur. He died in 1935 at the age of 59. It is perhaps thanks to his father's legacy that Meinrad Schütter took a keen interest in history, politics and world affairs. As a regular reader of newspapers – several a day in fact – Schütter kept himself abreast of the latest news. Shortly before his death, he remarked that he would give anything to be able to argue politics again with his old compatriots in Chur.

When one travels by train eastwards from Zurich, the railway line divides in Sargans, taking a southerly route to Chur and the Bündner Oberland, and an easterly route to Austria, winding its way through the Arlberg massif to Innsbruck and then on to Vienna. High above the city

---

[2] Where not otherwise indicated, Schütter's recollections quoted in this book were made over the course of many conversations with me in the late 1990s and early 2000s.

The Obertor and Ochsenplatz in Chur, c. 1900

of Sargans, the local castle stands imposingly on its rocky hill – one of the most famous mediaeval fortresses in the region and an important stronghold of the Swiss Army during the Second World War. Like all the other castles in the area, its exposed position allowed it to dominate a long stretch of the Rhine Valley. In the heyday of the minnesingers and the

Joseph Schütter, c. 1930

troubadours, Walther von der Vogelweide might well have been a guest there on his travels from Vienna to the north. One cannot choose the epoch into which one is born, but Schütter always felt a kinship with the Middle Ages, its sacred and secular music and its poetry, and also felt particularly attached to this castle (though he imagined himself more as an erudite mediaeval scholar than as a pugnacious knight). In his final years, he took especial delight in interrupting his usual route of travel from Chur to Zurich in order to sit in the castle restaurant, gazing across the valley to the little village of Vilters – preferably while consuming a glass (or several) of red wine.

From Sargans, the Rhine flows down to the Austrian border and the province of Vorarlberg. On the Austrian, eastern bank of the river lie the neighbouring villages of Klaus and Götzis (only 25 miles northeast of Sargans as the crow flies), which was where the family lived of Emilie Hegner (1887–1966), Schütter's mother. Her grandfather seems to have been something of an adventurous figure. He was a teacher and wine-merchant in Klaus, where he ran either the 'Hecht' or 'Adler' hotel (the records are unclear on this point). Around the time of the second Polish uprising against the Russians that began in 1863, appeals for the liberation of Poland fell on fertile ground in Switzerland, Austria and elsewhere. Schütter's great-grandfather sympathised with the rebels and began smuggling weapons to Poland in wine barrels. But his activities were revealed when one of these barrels fell from a railway carriage in Bregenz, laying bare its unexpected content as it clattered down. Great-grandfather Gut immediately fled with his family to Chur, opening a restaurant on the Kornplatz. But he travelled to Munich soon afterwards, never to be seen again, leaving behind his wife and three daughters: Mathilde, Alberta and Sophie. The family later ran another restaurant, the Franziskaner on the Ochsenplatz in Chur.

The youngest of these sisters, Sophie Gut, born in 1857, went to Florence at a young age to work as a governess to the two daughters of a wealthy American who was able to employ none other than Franz Liszt and Francesco Paolo Tosti for their music lessons (which naturally became another story that Schütter delighted in telling: his grandmother had met Liszt). Sophie returned home with a good knowledge of Italian, and proceeded to marry Meinrad Hegner, a soap-boiler from Chur. They had no children. Sophie's sister Mathilde, by contrast, was now expecting an illegitimate child, after having been abandoned by its father, supposedly an architect by the name of Schock. Just like the father of Sophie and Mathilde, he now similarly disappeared without a trace – in this instance to Paris, so the story went.

Mathilde's child, Emilie, was born in a convent in Ems. The family tried their best to hide the fact of her birth, so she was promptly taken in by Mathilde's sister Sophie and passed off as her own. Everyone was sworn to absolute secrecy about this arrangement. Thus, from the very start, Emilie Hegner grew up believing that Sophie was her mother, not her aunt. Her biological mother, Mathilde Gut, later married a hotelier from Davos. But he had little interest in children, and the sisters kept to their arrangement. However, their world finally came crashing down at the civil marriage ceremony of Emilie Hegner to Joseph Johann Schütter, because the truth came out when their respective birth certificates had to be presented at the registry office. The unfortunate bride was utterly unprepared for the shock, and promptly succumbed to a nervous breakdown. Meinrad Schütter was the first-born of Emilie and Joseph, thus making Sophie Hegner, *née* Gut, his 'wrong' grandmother (incidentally, Schütter never tired of complaining about the 'cowardice' of the men in the Gut family). For Schütter and his brother Joseph, Mathilde Albrecht-Gut – their real grandmother – was simply 'the aunt from Götzis'.

Emilie's biological mother, Mathilde, did not attend her daughter's wedding. She ran the 'Viola' boarding house for tuberculosis patients in Davos and moved to Vienna in 1919, though not before buying a small house in Götzis that Emilie Schütter inherited after her mother's death; it was sold off by her family in 1937.

3
Childhood and Early Youth

Meinrad Schütter's mother Emilie had grown up in the loving care of Sophie Hegner, and Meinrad was himself full of stories about his 'wrong' grandmother that reflected the admiration, respect and love that he felt for her. She comes across as a capable, intelligent, energetic woman. An eye ailment prompted her doctor to advise a move to a greener environment, and so she bought a piece of land at Lürlibad in Chur, on the edge of the area known as the 'Fürstenwald', from where she had a splendid view of the upper Rhine, the Bündner Oberland, and the Calanda Mountain on the other side of the valley whose peak is covered in snow for most of the year.

It was here that Sophie Hegner built the chalet 'Waldegg' in 1899 (it still exists). She then turned it into a guesthouse called Klein-Waldegg, with a restaurant and a large garden that was later Meinrad Schütter's childhood paradise. Sophie Hegner was what might today be termed an emancipated woman, organising and supervising the building of her guesthouse on her own. Schütter later recalled:

> The guests of the boarding house at that time were all lovers of the kind of Romantic landscapes and nature that were already in the process of disappearing. There was the writer Karl Bleibtreu, a co-founder of the naturalist literary movement in Berlin, the medical professor [Wilhelm] His from Basel who worked in Leipzig (a friend of Johannes Brahms), then the conductor of the famous Mendelssohn Choir in Frankfurt,[1] and Dr [Josef] Jörger, the head of the nearby psychiatric clinic Waldhaus in Chur.

The Klein-Waldegg guesthouse became Schütter's real home during his childhood and early youth. The immediate proximity of the mountain forest with its summer scents and winter snow awakened a love of nature in him – not surprising, given his Romantic, poetic bent. It was there that he could go to seek silence and solitude – his 'Eichendorff idyll', as he often called it, after the early Romantic German poet who had sung the praises of forests and meadows a century earlier. There, in the company of fox, hare and squirrel, Schütter created his own microcosm – an interior space that was inaccessible to the outside world, even to those closest to him. This Romantic 'forest solitude' became his place of retreat and a point

---

[1] Presumably August Grüter (1841–1911), from 1893 to 1909 the conductor of the Cäcilien-Verein in Frankfurt am Main.

Schütter's 'wrong' grandmother
Sophie Hegner, c. 1895

of escape, and he later returned to it time and again in his songs and his Piano Concerto.

Nor was Schütter a stranger to the world of ghosts and dream spirits – and here, the legendary Scaläratobel ravine near his grandparents' chalet may have been a contributory factor. It was reputedly the place where the unredeemed souls of Chur's deceased citizens would roam at the

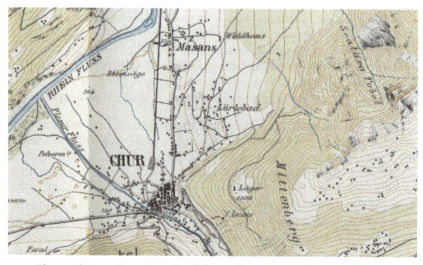

Chur and its environs, in a detail from a late-nineteenth-century map,
showing the Rhein to the north-west, the Scaläratobel ravine to the north-east
and Lürlibad, where Sophie Hegner built the chalet 'Waldegg'.

'Klein-Waldegg', built by Meinrad Schütter's grandmother in 1899

witching hour of midnight. Schütter's imagination conjured up all manner of ghostly scenes, and he later returned to the topic in his piano music. Romanticism, its metaphors and foreshadowings of things to come played a fundamental role in shaping the mind of the composer; it was here that his poetical side came to life. Schütter loved great poetry; to him it was essential for life itself, and it was why, as a composer, he returned time and again to song-composition.

In 1911, one year after Meinrad, his brother Joseph was born. The family called him 'Pepi'. One of their frequent playmates was Cilly Keel (later Cilly Bove), who lived to over 100. She was the daughter of Adolf Keel, the co-founder of the 'Cäcilienverein' in Chur, a mixed choir whose members included Meinrad's parents, Joseph and Emilie – indeed, Emilie supposedly had a lovely voice, and often sang solo parts. Cilly Keel recalled Meinrad's mother as being very beautiful but a cold woman, 'with a small heart', though she described Sophie Hegner by contrast as a woman possessed of deep kindness.[2] Emilie often preferred leaving her children with Sophie Hegner, as she herself didn't have much clue what to do with them. This apparent lack of maternal feelings on Emilie's part seems to have been at the root of Schütter's difficult relationship with his mother.

---

[2] Conversation with me, 11 June 2007, in Chur. The following quotations from Cilly Keel's reminiscences are also taken from this conversation.

From the left: Meinrad Schütter on the lap of Sophie Hegner;
his grandfather Hegner; Joseph Schütter; Joseph ('Pepi')
on the lap of Emilie Schütter.

Pepi and Meinrad Schütter, c. 1913

Sophie Hegner was very religious – so much so that she even set up an altar at home in case the weather was bad on a Sunday and the children couldn't get to church. Then she herself would stay with them, pray with them and read to them. Pepi had a more delicate constitution, a fact for which Meinrad was blamed by his mother early on. She would complain bitterly that he, the first-born, had taken all her strength, 'and there was nothing left for Pepi'.[3] Schütter must have taken this reproach to heart as a child, as he felt responsible for his brother for the rest of his life, always doing his best to protect him whenever he could.

When Meinrad began attending the Hofschule in Chur – the Catholic Church of the Bishopric, staffed by nuns – he felt that he had been snatched away from paradise. He found the syllabus easy enough, though it did not interest him much. When Pepi began school a year after him, he had a hard time of it, and so Meinrad – according to his own account – decided to repeat a year in order to be placed in the same class as his brother and help him on a daily basis.

Pepi later completed an apprenticeship as a painter, like their father, though after the latter's death, the resultant financial turmoil led to the bankruptcy of the family business. A stomach ailment caused Pepi to switch to banking. He married in 1952; after his wife's death, he lived alone, with diabetes subsequently being added to his ailments. He died a

[3] *Ibid.*

Klein-Waldegg with its German internee soldiers
during the First World War.

sudden death in 1988, which was a shock to Meinrad, not least because it
was a suspected suicide.

Schütter summed up their early years as follows:

> Pepi was born in Chur in 1911, and he and I spent a uniquely happy
> childhood. Above the city, at the edge of the forest, with a view of the
> Upper Rhine Valley towards the Gotthard Pass, surrounded by forests
> with their Eichendorffian Romanticism, far away from the hurly-burly of
> the world, the little guesthouse called Klein-Waldegg still stands today.
> It was in this natural setting that our highly musical mother sang songs to
> us by Robert Schumann, Johannes Brahms, Richard Strauss – and already
> Othmar Schoeck.
>
> The primary school was more than half an hour away. Its constraints
> and religious narrow-mindedness pleased neither of us very much,
> especially since it alienated us from our paradise back in nature. This
> stupidest of centuries, as Oskar Kokoschka once called the 20th, began
> very early with the First World War. German internees, unarmed but in
> uniform, were spread all over German-speaking Switzerland, and for
> several years they were the saviour of the guesthouse. When they all left
> Klein-Waldegg at the end of the war, that's when the financial downfall
> began.

Klein-Waldegg was sold soon afterwards.

Schütter's intense musicality was noticed early by those around him.
He was first given piano lessons, and then organ lessons, too. Nevertheless,

Pepi and Meinrad Schütter in Arosa, 1924

when his tenth birthday arrived, he was unsure whether to ask for a piano or a cow, since he also wanted to become a farmer. He always found cows to be extraordinarily beautiful – and highly musical, too. In later life, when he went on mountain hikes, he would often sing to them, starting with alphorn and ländler melodies, then moving on to his own music. And the ponderous animals would inevitably lift themselves up and make their way slowly to the source of this novel disturbance of their everyday ruminating monotony. Schütter, ultimately surrounded by them, was always enthusiastic about his success, and argued that it proved Stravinsky's claim that only children and animals could understand his music.

One of Schütter's most important early role models was the conductor Ernst Schweri Sr, from Chur, who had studied with the renowned conductor Felix Mottl in Munich before returning to impart something of the aura of the great Austro-German music tradition to his native Chur. Schütter was taken by his parents to Ernst Schweri's choral concerts in Chur from an early age. They were a revelation to him, and left a deep impression at a time when Schütter's musical sensibilities were as yet 'uncultivated land'.

As a stubborn adolescent, Schütter's strict Catholic upbringing and the rules to be observed at school were increasingly felt by him to be unnecessary restrictions he might ignore when he felt like it. Reprimands and disciplinary measures on the part of the school authorities were not long in coming. His parents had no better idea of how to cope than to send their difficult son to a religious retreat in the holidays. The venue was the Catholic-run Johannes-Stift in nearby Zizers. The recollections of Schütter's friends vary as to the duration of his stay there. Some assumed it had been for a week, while others recalled a period of several months, and yet another believed it to have been no less than three years. Schütter himself spoke of the experience as having lasted a few days, which probably corresponded to the facts, and seems confirmed by his own slightly cynical remarks about this period of his life. In the sermons and so-called tuition that he endured there, he encountered a one-sided, backward-looking church that sought to manipulate young people by preventing them from thinking for themselves. The images it offered up of a personified, vengeful God and hosts of saints in a pseudo-Hellenistic panoply of heaven suddenly assumed clarity and transparency for Schütter where before they had existed in a blur of naïve, childish perception. His inner sense of protest and resentment was only magnified by what he saw as sheer stupidity, and the consequence was withdrawal. He stayed away from the sermons, locked himself in his cell and composed his first song. From one moment to the next, he claimed, he knew that he would become a musician. This moment of illumination provided him with the orientation he needed. Schütter never severed his attachment to the Catholic faith, but remained a critical observer and engaged with questions of religious philosophy throughout his life.

Zizers had not fulfilled his parents' hopes of turning him into an insightful, docile son, but instead had become a trigger experience showing him what he might become – while leaving him no less 'difficult' than before. It had been for him a kind of banishment that brought about a clear realisation that he must build his own 'house in the spirit', and that he would need only this and nothing else. He had already decided that striving for worldly possessions was not something that would occupy him much in his life.

As he discovered great literature and poetry and the horizons of his thinking expanded, Schütter moved away from his grandmother's simple piety to a kind of world-encompassing, nature-based religiosity instead that was more akin to the beliefs of Goethe. He began to traverse mental

Joseph Schütter on a snowy path surrounded by pine trees covered in snow.

The first-ever car trip for the local dignitaries of Chur,
from Chur to Davos, c. 1923.
To the left, standing behind the car, is Joseph Schütter

boundaries for the first time – indeed, the idea of crossing boundaries and of an itinerant existence both metaphorical and literal became of crucial importance to him. He 'carried his own house' with him everywhere, so to speak.

Schütter attended the cantonal high school in Chur, followed by the local teacher-training college. By a stroke of luck, Antoine-Elisée Cherbuliez,[4] later a lecturer in musicology at the University of Zurich, was at the time still living and working in Chur. Schütter already played the organ very well, and was sometimes allowed to play the large Romantic organ in Chur Cathedral that had been built by Friedrich Goll. Cherbuliez became aware of him, recognised his talent and began giving him music-theory lessons while Schütter was still at the local college of education. He also recommended that Schütter pursue his music studies at the Zurich Conservatoire (today the Zurich University of Music). He accordingly enrolled there in 1930, despite initial resistance from his parents.

Even before Cherbuliez's interventions in Schütter's first intrepid attempts at composition, he had written a string quartet to which he later often made jocular reference, as it was full of well-nigh insurmountable

---

[4] Antoine-Elisée Cherbuliez (1888–1964), one of the first Swiss musicologists, studied organ with Albert Schweitzer and composition with Max Reger; he trained initially as a civil engineer before turning to musicology, which he taught at the University of Zurich in later life. (There was also a Swiss economist of the same name, 1797–1869.)

technical difficulties, despite being intended for performance at his high school. Schütter handed out the parts for it to the most talented instrumentalists among his peers – one of them Philipp Zinsli, who later became a close friend. Their efforts to master it were inevitably characterised by a sense of schoolboy reluctance, and it was soon declared to be absolutely unplayable. Worst of all, they claimed that it didn't sound 'beautiful' at all. Although such a complaint would have amused or even encouraged him in later life, Schütter reacted by destroying his quartet along with all his other attempts at composition from this time. It was left to Antoine Cherbuliez, and after him the teachers of the Zurich Conservatoire, to bring order to the budding composer's unrefined thoughts.

4
Friends of Youth

It was during his years at school and college that Meinrad Schütter developed his love of literature and history, especially of the poetry of the major German Romantics. 'My essays on Eichendorff at teacher-training college were a triumph', he used to recall with delight. It was at about this time that his two closest friendships came about: with Emanuel Bernard (1911–87), whom Schütter knew from school, and with the poet Nandor Währing (1908–57), a Hungarian immigrant.

Bernard was born a year later than Schütter, who recalled the early years of their acquaintance not long after his friend's death in 1987:

> For six months we sat at neighbouring desks in the teacher-training college in Chur. Then he suddenly disappeared [...]. I later spotted him at the Chur City Theatre, working as an extra on stage. He was also able to recite Goethe's *Faust I* from memory [...]. His father was horrified at his son, withdrew him from college and set him to work in his installation company.

Bernard went on to study classical philology in Zurich and set up his own private school there, the 'Mittelschule Dr. Bernard'. He and Schütter renewed their friendship in Zurich after the Second World War: 'the older we became, the closer we were', Schütter recalled, 'we'd exchange reminiscences that were vivid, though they became increasingly monosyllabic'; 'we differed in our approach to religion. He was a rational Huguenot [...] while I was a musician and Baroque by nature [...] and an adherent of the colours and sounds of the Counter-Reformation'. In one thing, however, they agreed, namely in the narrow-mindedness of their native city; it was Bernard who once quipped that 'the best thing about Chur is the express train to Zurich'.

With Nandor Währing, by contrast, Schütter felt a deep spiritual kinship. Schütter generally cultivated a degree of equanimity, never uttering a harsh word about others, but also remaining reserved in his friendships. Währing was an exception – someone with whom Schütter felt able to discuss issues of existential import. He had arrived in Switzerland shortly after the First World War, when the Swiss 'Kinderhilfe' ('Children's Aid') transported a host of young people from Hungary who had been

Emanuel Bernard and Meinrad Schütter, 1981

deemed in need of respite from the widespread economic malaise that was sweeping the former Hapsburg Empire (their number also included Maria Stader, who later achieved international fame as a concert soprano). Währing was placed in Chur, where as a teenager he became firm friends with Schütter and Emanuel Bernard. Schütter acknowledged that Währing possessed the broader intellect, and they often spent many hours at night discussing God and the world, sometimes on long walks through the woods outside Chur. It was Währing who introduced Schütter to the realms of philosophy and contemporary literature. 'Nandor Währing was the ideal friend for me at that time in godforsaken Chur', Schütter recalled in 2002.

Schütter had naturally grown up speaking the local Swiss German dialect, whereas Währing spoke a polished High German with a Hungarian accent. Both had a poetic bent and saw poetry as a form of expression that offered the widest possible freedom and intellectual independence. Thanks to their frequent conversations, Schütter too grew fond of High German, taking delight in archaic turns of phrase reminiscent of the language of Luther. He spoke in a soft baritone – with occasional, theatrical eruptions – and in a distinctive rhythm with a slight eastern timbre, the latter no doubt a result of Währing's influence. Both he and Währing cultivated a striking prose style in their letters.

On a visit to me in Basel in 1993, Schütter handed over Nandor Währing's posthumous papers with the urgent request that, after his

Meinrad Schütter at the organ, c. 1928

Nandor Währing and Meinrad Schütter, c. 1929

death, I should 'do something' for his friend and his work. This Währing 'archive' comprised a small package of three disintegrating notebooks full of handwritten poems in Hungarian, plus a number of thin, typewritten sheets of airmail paper with German translations, and a small bundle of letters, picture postcards and other cards from Währing to Schütter, all dating from after 1948. These documents were clearly of considerable importance to Schütter.

Schütter's side of the correspondence has sadly been lost, but Währing's letters alone enabled me to reconstruct their friendship. They cover a vast spectrum of topics, ranging from epistemology to winter coats. They also demonstrate how the euphoric friendship of their youth, when both were confident of finding their way as artists in the world, gave way inexorably in Währing's case to a loss of hope under the weight of political and personal events. These extant letters and cards chart the path of a man caught up in the machinery of war and persecution, ultimately perishing in it.

In the years 1937–39, both men endured existential crises. Schütter later recalled this time as follows:

> My grandmother Sophie was in the Marienheim [a home run by nuns in Chur], my father was dead, the family company bankrupt, my mother with some farmer or other (she had remarried), Pepi unemployed, me in Basel, then later in Rome. And then there was the narrow-minded

conservativism of Chur society, with me already a free thinker, always hanging out with this Hungarian, Nandor Währing, whose laughter seemed to mock the Philistines. They never liked him. Then there was the magistrate Eugen Dedual, to whom I dedicated one of my first songs back in 1933 ['Hochzeitslied: aus dem Jugoslawischen'], a friend of my father's, who said I ought to be put in a detention centre in Domleschg because I was a good-for-nothing! He later became a public prosecutor.

Nandor Währing's plight was even worse. After having spent many of the previous years in Switzerland, his residence permit was revoked and he had to leave the country. On 7 December 1937, he wrote to Schütter from Budapest: 'Take courage, courage, in these explosive times. Courage in spite of everything. You live in chaos, friend, rejoice! Form it!'. Two months later, in February 1938, he wrote again from Budapest: 'In these months I've not had enough money for postage stamps, because when I had scraped together enough […] I naturally had to invest it in the inevitable cigarettes' (though in this he knew he could rely on Schütter's sympathy, himself a heavy smoker until the end of his life). Währing offered sympathy for the bad reviews Schütter had experienced, and assured him that 'It will be a great year if Herr H. [Hitler] doesn't make it a year of doom!'. Währing begged repeatedly for money in these months, which Schütter dutifully sent, although his own income was very low in 1937. All the same, Währing managed to publish a slim volume of poetry in that year.

Schütter spent much of 1939 on a scholarship in Rome.[1] Währing visited him there, and from the dates he assigned to his poems one can deduce that he spent the ensuing war years there, too. The outbreak of war seems to have caused an interruption in their correspondence – Schütter naturally had to enlist in military service, and letters between them might well have been lost. After the war, Währing was interned, probably because he did not have valid residence documents. My endeavours to find out more about his whereabouts in these years have proven fruitless, though I know that he was sent from one Italian internment camp to another between 1948 and 1957, the last of them being in Aversa in southern Italy. Letters and cards from Währing to Schütter have survived from Rome and Fiesole from 1948 and 1949, then from the internment camps in Pagani (May 1950), Cava dei Tirreni (July 1950) and Capua. He writes of initial hopes of being allowed to remain officially in Italy, then of thoughts of emigration (a plan to leave for Paraguay failed to materialise), and of the dehumanising conditions in the camps. He keeps writing – in Cava dei Tirreni, for example, he embarked on a novella about Michelangelo.

---

[1] Discussed more fully on pp. 54–58, below.

Nandor Währing's pass for his failed emigration to Paraguay, 1948

There were flu outbreaks in the camps, nervous breakdowns and constant theft – and so Schütter sent clothes, coats and shoes. In late 1953, Währing – an anti-communist – was beaten up by political opponents. In 1954, he was given a three-month passport to be able to visit friends in Switzerland – but it all came to nothing when a local Swiss consul demanded that a mountain of forms and questionnaires be completed. This task took so long that the passport expired before Währing had surmounted all the administrative hurdles necessary for him to be able to use it. In 1956, Schütter received what would be Währing's last letter; he was now seriously ill, but still writing poems. Währing died in Aversa, just outside Naples, on 18 February 1957 at the age of 49. Schütter blamed himself for not having visited Währing there, as they both had hoped he would, though he simply did not have the money for the journey at the time.

In memory of Währing, Schütter wrote *Verbunkos* for piano duet. He later recalled:

> This piece arose from an encounter with two Hungarian dancers at Zurich Opera House, Ernö Vashegyi and his partner Vera Pasztor, who had fled their country after the uprising of 1956. They had lost all their sheet music during their flight and wanted to dance this old Hungarian song. They sang it to me, and I harmonised it together with a Czardas. At the same time, my friend, the writer Nandor Währing, died in an Italian refugee camp. This first version for piano four hands was written in his memory for the Zurich City Theatre, where Vashegyi and Pasztor danced at its first performance.

Schütter set three texts by Nandor Währing to music: *Abgrund* ('Abyss') for mezzo-soprano and piano in 1934/1939, *Zuspruch II* ('Assurance II') for mixed chorus in 1953 (revised in 1998), and then *Fragment* for voice and piano (which despite its name is not unfinished, but merely brief in duration) on 17 March 1957, after Schütter had learned of his friend's death. The original text was in Hungarian but seems not to have survived. In the German translation used by Schütter, it runs: 'Ich drück an das Herz dich, dorniges Leben, an das nackte Herz dich, qualvollschönes Leben und blick dir ins Aug' ('I press you to my heart, life of thorns, to my naked heart, you, agonisingly beautiful life, and look you in the eye').[2]

---

[2] This song is published in facsimile in Manfred Veraguth: '"Ich werde dieses Bündnerparadies wohl zu behandeln wissen": der Nachlass Meinrad Schütter (1910–2006) im Stadtarchiv Chur', in *Bündner Monatsblatt: Zeitschrift für Bündner Geschichte, Landeskunde und Baukultur*, 2016, No. 3, pp. 343–51, here p. 349.

5
The 1930s: Early Works

At the age of nineteen, when the gramophone was still a relative rarity in Chur, Schütter heard a record of Mozart's Symphony in A major, K201, for the first-ever time. It was an experience that he never forgot, and although he later declared that he must have been 'inexplicably delusional' that he still wanted to become a composer after hearing such wonderful music, his chosen path was at least one that would take this budding anti-bourgeois away from the narrow environment of his native Chur.

After lessons with Cherbuliez in 1930–31, Schütter followed his recommendation to audition for the Zurich Conservatoire. 'Volkmar Andreae [the director] accepted me into the Conservatoire on the strength of a savage Beethoven sonata', he later recalled. He studied piano, organ and composition in Zurich, commuting there and back every day. He cycled the seventeen miles from Chur to Sargans each morning, where he caught the morning train arriving from Vienna on its way to Zurich. The Sargans-Zurich railway line remains one of the most picturesque, romantic lines in all Switzerland, snaking its way through tunnels and sparse forests along the banks of Lake Walen, with the sheer cliffs of the Churfirsten mountain range rising up opposite (the same lake that had inspired Franz Liszt to his piano piece 'Au lac de Wallenstadt' during his Swiss 'pilgrimage' a century before Schütter). But it is hardly conducive for a daily commute. Schütter usually had to remain at the Conservatoire until the evening, but if he stayed to attend a concert in town, he would often miss the last slow train back to Sargans. All the same, he went to as many concerts as his finances would allow, and often saved money by sleeping on station benches. He later called these his 'heroic years'.

Andreae shared the directorship of the Zurich Conservatoire with one Carl Vogler (1874–1951), a local composer of conservative views and a powerful administrator who was also the President of the Swiss Musicians' Association. He and Schütter failed to get on from the start, for they were too different in their politics and their aesthetic. When the Schütter family business in Chur went bankrupt in 1935, leaving Meinrad unable to pay his tuition fees, Vogler insisted that he abandon his studies at the conservatoire – though not before agreeing to accept a Persian rug from Schütter's grandmother in lieu of unpaid fees.

The Zurich Conservatoire, c. 1930

Carl Vogler's letter to Meinrad Schütter of 30 January 1940,
confirming his rejection by the Swiss Musicians' Association

Four years later, after Alexander Schaichet had conducted the first performance of Schütter's *Five Variants and Metamorphosis* in Zurich, Schütter applied to join the Swiss Musicians' Association but, given that the association was dominated by Vogler, it was hardly surprising that Schütter was rejected. Vogler wrote:

> Dear Sir,
> the Board of the Swiss Musicians' Association has recently raised the bar for admission quite considerably. Apart from the musical values to which you adhere, other matters have also come into consideration, such as the issue of your studies at the Zurich Conservatoire and especially your departure from that same institution. I shall have the secretary send you the application forms, though I herewith confirm quite openly that I shall oppose your admission for as long as the Zurich Conservatoire remains unsatisfied as to the financial demands that it has against you [...].[1]

Schütter's reply is no longer extant, though it clearly confirmed all of Vogler's suspicions about him, for he in turn replied as follows:

---

[1] Letter from Vogler dated 3 August 1939.

thank you most sincerely for your kind letter. It is extraordinarily
important to us to have received proof from you personally that we did
well in not accepting you into our Association, for decency is also a quality
that musicians can hardly do without.[2]

While neutral Switzerland was trying to negotiate a path for itself on
the shifting European landscape, Vogler was one of many whose politics
were as conservative as their aesthetic – he attended events in Germany
organised by the Nazi-sponsored 'Ständiger Rat',[3] and personally solicited
information from the Swiss Ministry of the Interior on the communist
affiliations of such musicians as Hermann Scherchen.[4] Schütter did not
forget this early rejection, and in later years refused requests to join the
Association until finally convinced to do so in 1993 by its then president,
Martin Derungs, a fellow native of Chur.

Leaving the Conservatoire without finishing his studies left Schütter
feeling bitter, but his time spent there would seem to have been remarkably
beneficial, as there now followed several years of intensive compositional
activity, beginning with songs and culminating in his first works for
chamber ensemble and for string orchestra. Right from the start, Schütter's
primary role-models were to be found in the Germanic tradition. He
admired Beethoven's 'proletarian pathos' and was especially fascinated
by Wagner, though his passionate enthusiasm was later tempered by
ambivalence on account of how Wagner was misappropriated by the Third
Reich. On a long hike that he took with me on the occasion of his 90th
birthday, Schütter recalled his initial astonishment when his friend Nandor
Währing once insisted on reading the libretto of *Die Walküre*. 'We listened
to him, his critical young friends, and laughed ourselves silly! Wagner's
libretti – how could you just *read* them!?! What an idea. And yet Wagner
was a poet. There are passages that are grandiose!'.

As a poetry-lover, it was natural that Schütter should compose Lieder.
His output is notable for two major periods of continuous creativity: from
1931 to 1940, and again from around 1985 to 2005, with song-composition
playing a major role in each. As a composer of Lieder, Schütter's early ideal
was his Swiss compatriot Othmar Schoeck. Schütter recalled his mother
singing songs by Schoeck when he was a child, and he later admired how
Schoeck was able to identify with his poets and get 'under their skin'. He
loved Schoeck's early, proto-cyclic *Zwölf Eichendorff-Lieder*, Op. 30, and
would later enthuse about his large-scale song-cycles of the 1940s, *Unter*

---

[2] Letter from Vogler dated 30 January 1940.
[3] Minutes of the Swiss Musicians' Association committee meeting of 22 April 1937, held today by the
Bibliothèque cantonale et universitaire – Lausanne.
[4] Minutes of the Association committee meeting of 29 January 1939.

Sternen, Op. 55 (to texts by Gottfried Keller), and *Das stille Leuchten*, Op. 60 (C. F. Meyer). Schütter tended to asymmetry when he composed his vocal lines, and his songs of the 1930s already demonstrate a high degree of independence between the voice and piano. In stylistic terms, it is clear that the impact exerted by Schoeck was soon joined by that of Schoenberg and Berg.

As with Schoeck, Schütter preferred to set poetry either by personal friends or by the classic German writers – though his selection of the latter extended further into the twentieth century than was the case with Schoeck, with settings of Rilke, Walser, Nelly Sachs and others; and quite unlike Schoeck, Schütter also had a keen interest in Rumansh poetry. In fact, Schütter's acknowledged *œuvre* begins with a Rumansh song: *Dumonda*, composed in 1931 to a poem by Gian Caduff (Ex. 1). Its origins lay a year earlier, in 1930, when Schütter was waiting for a lesson with Antoine Cherbuliez. A young, black-haired student with a fine, bright soprano voice was having a singing lesson, and she caught Schütter's attention when she explained cheekily to her teacher that she hadn't been practising. Her name was Claudia Mengelt. They thereafter became better acquainted, the attraction proved mutual, and it was she who commissioned *Dumonda*, convinced as she was of his talent and keen to encourage him. It was his first paid commission. It is late-Romantic in style, but with a folk-like tone. Looking back many years later, Schütter quipped that it sounds as if it had been composed by a mountain dweller who still thought in Latin, but had already heard Richard Strauss. *Dumonda* received its first performance on Swiss Radio in 1936, sung by Claudia Mengelt, accompanied by the composer.

Schütter's next song was *Hochzeitslied* ('Wedding Song'; 1933), to a text translated from the Serbo-Croat, which is clearly influenced by Slavic folk-rhythms and melody. It was followed that same year by *Als er seiner Magdalis nichts zum Grünen Donnerstag schenken konnte* ('When he was unable to give his Magdalis any gifts on Maundy Thursday'), to a poem by the Baroque Silesian writer Johann Christian Günther (1695–1723), whose reputation as a man of passionate excess fascinated Schütter.[5] The motoric motion in the piano accompaniment, and the emotional coolness of the song overall suggest the impact of the Neo-Classical movement. The songs *Vorfrühling* ('Early Spring'; 1934) to a text by Max Dauthendey, and the two settings of Rainer Maria Rilke, *Herbsttag* ('Autumn Day';

---

[5] Günther's brief life (he was only 27 when he died) was one of drunken dissipation: he failed to complete studies in medicine, and a recommendation from a friend to Frederick Augustus II, Elector of Saxony (he was also Augustus III of Poland and Grand Duke of Lithuania), came to naught when Günther turned up to the audience drunk. Goethe was one of many later literary figures who found much to admire in his poetry.

Ex. 1

Ca-ra ro-sa cotsch-ni-na,   o gi ti a   mi: ha la mat-ta ca-ri-na getg nuot-zun a

ti?   cru siu maun a-mu-rei-vel dal rom tei ha__ rut?

Ha igl egl bun-ta-dei-vel cru-schiu lu dal tut?   Has buc__

viu   ell' eg-lia-da,   la__ bras-cla d'a-mur,

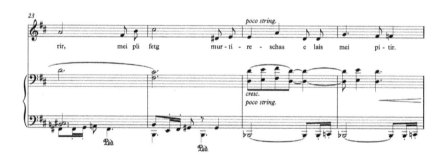

1934) and *Ernste Stunde* ('Serious Hour'; 1935), are only loosely tonal, whereas *Morgentau* ('Morning Dew'), *Die müden Sterne* ('The weary stars') and *Südliches Glockenspiel* ('Southern Chimes'), all settings of the Swiss Expressionist poet Karl Stamm, date from 1934 and are linear in style and Neo-Baroque in character. Schütter remarked later: 'The poet Karl Stamm (1890–1919), who died all too soon, was very important to me in my youth. His life reflected both the spiritual situation and the general misery that reigned during and after the First World War'. The year 1936 saw Schütter compose the brief song *Vor der Ernte* ('Before the Harvest'; 1936), to a text by Martin Greif (1839–1911), which is unusual in his *œuvre* in that it also exists in a version for voice and string quartet.

Schütter's work as a choral conductor and organist also led him to compose a number of sacred songs, such as *Kyrie* (1938) to a text by Martin Schmid (1889–1971), who was one of the leading poets of Graubünden in his day, the Director of the Teachers' Training College in Chur and one of Schütter's own teachers in 1927–29. Other songs of these years, such as three brief songs to late-Mediaeval texts[6] composed in 1933 and 1934, belong among those works that Schütter once described as 'short, little songs composed spontaneously for domestic use'. Similar occasional

---

[6] Schütter later grouped these together with a fourth song composed in 1995 to form the *Vier alte Spielmannsweisen* ('Four Old Minstrel Songs'); *cf.* p. 163, below.

works exist in his output of chamber music: short, often aphoristic works for all manner of instrumental combinations. But Schütter's first larger-scale work of chamber music is also a song: the *Serenade* for soprano and string trio, composed in 1934 and revised in 1970, which comprises two instrumental outer movements and a weightier middle movement that is a setting of Hermann Hesse's poem 'Dreistimmige Musik' ('Three-part Music'). All three movements are linked motivically and are characterised by a free-tonal polyphony in which Schütter endeavours to avoid any obvious late-Romanticism. This work was not given its premiere until 31 January 1986 in Chur, with Helen Keller (soprano) accompanied by the Munich String Trio.

Schütter now also began to get opportunities to perform his songs, primarily in his home canton. It is impossible to reconstruct his concert activities of these years with any accuracy, because many programmes have not survived. On 4 February 1936 in St Martin's Church in Chur, for example, Eva Fein (mezzo-soprano) and Lucas Barth (bass) sang Schütter's two Rilke settings and two of his sacred songs, and eight days later on 12 February 1936, Barbara Wiesmann-Hunger (soprano) and Alfred Zäch (piano), two well-known musicians in Chur, gave a concert to a packed audience in the Chur Volkshaus that featured songs and piano pieces by Schütter, including the song *Vorfrühling*, which was dedicated to the singer.

Another concert in the Volkshaus, given two years later on 23 January 1938, saw Claudia Mengelt, Lucas Barth and Schütter himself perform several of his songs and his Piano Sonata, and resulted in an extensive review by his former teacher Antoine Cherbuliez in *Der Freie Rätier*. He pondered whether the composer was the best interpreter of his own music, and noted that the essential prerequisites for a good composer include diligence and serious study – two qualities that he felt were lacking in Schütter – though he nevertheless admitted that Schütter had his own way of doing things:

> only a strong, serious character can lead the seething chaos in the soul of a gifted musician through all dangers to reach a serene creativity [...]. These opinions and reservations rose up once again when listening to the compositions of this undoubtedly gifted composer, who is at present the most extreme modernist among the young composers of Graubünden.[7]

Cherbuliez went on to write the following (it is not clear to which work he is referring): 'time and again, he begins to reveal more clarity and grip in his structures, but overall the music tends to disintegrate too much into pieces of a mosaic'. He here identifies Schütter's tendency to fragmentation that would remain a feature of his music. But his assessment of the songs

[7] Antoine Cherbuliez, review, *Der Freie Rätier*, 24 January 1938.

Claudia Mengelt (later Claudia Schütter) in Splügen in the mid-1930s

was positive overall, and he closed by saying: 'May he succeed more and more in taming and training his own nature and talent'. Notwithstanding his criticism, Cherbuliez always remained favourably disposed towards Schütter and his music.

Schütter began sketching a symphony in 1937, but set it aside to write his *Five Variants and Metamorphosis* for string orchestra. It was the first orchestral piece that he completed, and his most significant work of the decade. It was requested by the Zurich Chamber Orchestra and its conductor, Alexander Schaichet, to whom it is also dedicated. Schaichet was a Russian cellist who had been stranded in Zurich by chance when the First World War broke out, and remained in Switzerland thereafter, setting up the first-ever chamber orchestra in the country in 1920 (the Zurich Chamber Orchestra) and becoming an advocate for music both old and new.

Schütter had originally sent Schaichet a set of piano variations on the Advent carol 'Macht hoch die Tür, die Tor macht weit' ('Fling wide the door'), at which Schaichet had suggested orchestrating them, and was also responsible for including the word 'metamorphosis' in the title. The idea of 'metamorphosis' as a formal principle in which an idea progresses successively through different degrees of transformation was one that occupied Schütter early on, and this work encompasses a network of motivic references that shift and alter constantly. Schütter began work on the orchestral version in 1938.

The exchange of letters between Schaichet and Schütter reveal Schaichet's warmth and sympathy for the fate of young composers. In his first extant letter, dated 15 June 1938, he thanked Schütter for the dedication and explained his conditions for its performance: providing a clean copy of the score and all the parts. In a subsequent letter, Schaichet gently but insistently hinted that Schütter ought to devote himself to 'putting his thoughts down on paper', for otherwise his 'beautiful thoughts' would 'become blurred'. Nor did Schaichet refrain from rebuking Schütter about inaccuracies and errors in the orchestral parts, which Schaichet himself then had to 'eradicate', nor about the confusion caused by his using 'different paper formats, different inks etc.!'.[8] He warned that such carelessness could damage a composer's reputation, and put his finger on a trait of Schütter's that remained a fundamental characteristic of the man and his work: a lack of external order that often culminated in chaos. On the reverse of the letter containing Schaichet's complaints, Schütter himself noted: 'Better to err on important paths than to be in error in a

---

[8] Undated letter from Schaichet to Schütter, presumably late 1938 or early 1939, held today by the Stadtarchiv Chur.

conventional, insignificant, lifeless way'. But all the same, it must be said that Schütter cultivated disorder throughout the rest of his life, even to the point of sloppiness in his scores, prompting performers to complain often about passages that had been struck out or pasted over or revised copiously using ink over correcting fluid.

These *Five Variants and Metamorphosis* were given their first performance on 30 March 1939 in the Main Hall of the Zurich Conservatoire. The same programme also included two more Swiss world premieres: the *Concerto for Piano and Chamber Orchestra*, Op. 72, by Fred C. Hay[9] and the *Toccata for String Orchestra*, Op. 55, by Willy Burkhard.[10] Schütter was in Rome when his new work was given its first performance. The committee of the Zurich Chamber Orchestra offered him fifty francs to enable him to return to Zurich for the concert, but Schütter stayed put. Schaichet sent him a lukewarm review by Willi Schuh in the *Neue Zürcher Zeitung* (in which Schuh complained about the lack of personality in Schütter's style)[11] and added in hand: 'Given the attitude in the local press to everything UNKNOWN, you've come off very leniently. I'm delighted about it'. In the *Neue Zürcher Nachrichten*, the reviewer 'ee' was a little more positive, describing Schütter as an 'honest man and a respectable artist […]. The clear sound of the orchestra and the striking bass part reveal a conscientious effort'.[12] Schütter later recalled reading these reviews 'in the comforting proximity of the revolving copy of the "Venus de Milo" in the Vatican'.

In 1940, Schütter sent the score of his *Five Variants and Metamorphosis* to Hermann Scherchen (1891–1966), the chief conductor of the Winterthur City Orchestra whose left-wing politics had made him an exile in Switzerland since the Nazi ascendancy in 1933. He replied: 'I'd like to get to know other orchestral music [of yours] at a later date'.

These initial contacts with musicians such as Schaichet and Scherchen were of considerable importance for the young composer, offering him

---

[9] The Swiss composer and conductor Frederick Charles Hay (1888–1945) was born in Basel and studied medicine before devoting himself to music, counting among his teachers Hans Huber in Basel, Charles-Marie Widor in Paris and Robert Fuchs and Franz Schalk in Vienna. He was active as a conductor in Bern and Geneva and taught musicology at the University of Geneva. His orchestral works include *Heaven and Earth*, *Der Dom* ('The Cathedral') and, besides this work for piano, concertos for oboe, violin and viola.

[10] Willy Burkhard (1900–55) was born in Leubringen in Canton Bern and studied with Robert Teichmüller and Sigfrid Karg-Elert in Leipzig, Walter Courvoisier in Munich and Max d'Ollone in Paris. He composed in almost every genre but was known primarily for his Protestant choral music (such as his oratorio *Das Gesicht Jesajahs* ('The Face of Isaiah')). He was also one of the most prominent Swiss composition teachers of his time (his students included Klaus Huber, Rudolf Kelterborn and Meinrad Schütter – whose tuition is discussed on pp. 59–60, below).

[11] Willi Schuh, 'Neue Schweizer Musik', *Neue Zürcher Zeitung*, Vol. 160, No. 587, 'Second Sunday edition', 2 April 1939.

[12] 'ee' (Hermann Leeb), 'Zürcher Konzerte', *Neue Zürcher Nachrichten*, Vol. 35, No. 83, 8 April 1939.

an incentive and hope for the future. Scherchen in particular was a highly gifted conductor, generally regarded as critical and uncompromising. In 1945 he was appointed the chief conductor of the Zurich Radio Orchestra (officially named the 'Studio Orchestra Beromünster'), and was a vital pioneer and promoter of new music in Switzerland. He conducted Schütter's *Fuge* in 1946 in his radio-concert series 'Das neue Werk' ('New Works') and it enjoyed a very warm reception (Schütter renamed it *Ricercare* upon revising it in 1952). The weekly Zurich newspaper *Die Weltwoche* praised its novel conception and noted that 'the influence of Hindemith, which has otherwise become inevitable, is not perceptible in Schütter's music. His orchestral sound has more the colour of recent Stravinsky'.[13] Scherchen followed this performance that same year with the *Five Variants and Metamorphosis* (in a revised version), also in the series 'Das neue Werk', and again with the Studio Orchestra Beromünster.

After leaving the Zurich Conservatoire, Schütter travelled widely in Switzerland and the neighbouring countries, primarily Austria and Italy. He accompanied the singer Getulio de Ronzi on tour to Vaduz, Bad Ischl and Venice, performing opera arias alongside piano pieces of his own. But he also travelled about, which meant playing in bars and restaurants to pay his way. He busked thus through Basel in 1937, and even toured as the pianist of a Cossack band (he was made up so as not to stand out, and later claimed that his disguise made him look more 'Cossack' than any of the others). During these lean years, he occasionally received small financial contributions from wealthy families in his native Chur.[14] He also spent his time educating himself further – studying scores and listening to as much music as possible. He did his best to attend Paul Sacher's chamber-orchestra concerts in Basel, and when he didn't have the money to buy a ticket (which happened often), he was allowed to listen from outside the doors of the hall instead. Finally, in 1938, Schütter's patrons in Chur procured him a one-year scholarship to Rome, for which Willy Burkhard also wrote a letter of recommendation.

---

[13] 'Vn' (Aline Valangin?) in *Die Weltwoche*. Undated newspaper clipping.
[14] Such as the family of Hans Weber in Chur.

6
Rome, 1939

Schütter's year in Rome was one of the most concentrated, productive periods in his life, and by all accounts a happy one, too, despite the meagre financial resources his scholarship offered and despite the cold, his unheated accommodation and a frugal diet. 'I took refuge from the cold on a church pew in Rome in January. The priest had early Mass and a lot of candles – and very soon the altar began to exude a little warmth', he recalled in 2005. Being in Rome gave him a liberating sense of being free of any outside commitments. The political situation, however, was becoming increasingly volatile: 'I often saw Mussolini's thickset figure, which fitted in well with the architecture of Rome'. He experienced the election of Eugenio Pacelli as Pope Pius XII, the same who throughout the war seemed to glide effortlessly across the political scene.

Schütter also attended as many concerts as he could in Rome. On 15 January 1939, for example, he heard Bartók's *Music for Strings, Percussion and Celesta* in the Teatro Adriano, with the Orchestra of Santa Cecilia conducted by Fernando Previtali. He was perplexed that the Roman audience was clearly divided in its response, since he found the experience unforgettable. Schütter also made contact with a Romanian singer, one Constanța Brancovici, whom he had already met back in Zurich and who was now studying in Rome. He began accompanying her on the piano, and it was by all accounts their deepening relationship that inspired Schütter to begin a series of new works including a 'Great Mass' (*Grosse Messe*) for mixed choir, soloists and organ, on which he worked again in 1950, 1970 and 1978. It is impossible to date all the sketches for the Mass (many have presumably been lost), though its Kyrie – one of the first movements to be completed – displays a tendency towards a serial treatment of the material in its avoidance of note-repetition in its horizontal lines. Schütter also now began planning an opera. His original plan was to base it on Jean-Baptiste Racine's tragedy *Bérénice*, set in ancient Rome, but he discarded this idea upon deciding that Racine's text was too 'literary'. At roughly the same time, he came across the story of Medea, which suited him better, and for which he now made initial sketches. Before setting to work, Schütter studied both the religious writings of the Hungarian philologist Károly Kerényi (1897–1973) and Friedrich Nietzsche's *The Birth of Tragedy from*

*Meinrad Schütter
in Rome, 1939*

the Spirit of Music. A letter from Willy Burkhard to Schütter of 7 November 1939, not long after his return from Rome, refers specifically to the latter, discussing the conflict between the Apollonian and the Dionysian. But just like Schütter's *Grosse Messe*, this work too would take several decades to complete.

While in Rome, Schütter also composed numerous chamber works, piano pieces and songs. Brancovici was the dedicatee of his Neo-Classical Piano Sonatina, an *Ave Maria* for soprano and organ/piano and the sonnet for soprano and chamber orchestra *Die Liebende schreibt* ('The lover writes'; Goethe), all composed in 1939.[1] It was also Brancovici's influence that prompted Schütter to incorporate folkloristic, Slavic motifs in his songs and piano works from this period – such as in the third and final movement of his Piano Sonatina (a work that later elicited the admiration of Paul Hindemith[2]).

When Schütter recalled his relationship with Brancovici many years later, he intimated that he had been convinced at the time that she might be his ideal partner – someone who could both inspire him and offer the criticism he needed. They even began making plans to go to Prague for

---

[1] *Die Liebende schreibt* was first performed in Chur on 5 May 1981 by Karin Ott, soprano, and the Camerata Zürich conducted by Räto Tschupp.
[2] Schütter's studies with Hindemith are discussed on pp. 67–71, below.

further studies. The course of world events would soon have thwarted them; but their relationship in any case now ended abruptly for other reasons. At some point during their stay in Rome, Schütter and Brancovici travelled to Bologna to give a concert. Schütter invited his Hungarian friend Nandor Währing to join them. He came, and promptly began an affair with Brancovici, who left Schütter. They did not meet again until he made another brief visit to Rome over a decade later, in 1953. He felt betrayed, but did not break off his friendship with Währing.

Having grown up more or less in the shadow of the Cathedral in Chur, music and religion were always inextricably linked for Schütter, and he remained an intermittent church organist into his old age. He was also fascinated by mysticism, religious ritual and the primordial power that he sensed in the sacred. During his time in Rome, he attended Masses and concerts in a myriad of churches in the city. He was often in the Square and Basilica of St Peter's ('God's concentrate', he called it), though its very splendour felt somewhat alienating to him, and led him to reconsider his own position towards the Church, especially in the political context of the day. He oscillated between scepticism, acceptance and doubt. In spite of having chafed under a strict Catholic upbringing, he never experienced any crisis of faith. Religion remained for him a 'conditio sine qua non', and it was only in the last decade of his life that the conflict between faith and unbelief re-emerged for him.

Schütter's scholarship was coming to an end, and he had to return to Switzerland. The mobilisation of the Swiss Army was announced only days before Hitler's invasion of Poland, which meant that Schütter, like every Swiss male, would soon have to report for military duty. But difficulties arose at Chiasso, the border point between Italy and Switzerland. His papers were invalid – presumably they were either incomplete or had expired – and he was refused entry. As a last resort, Schütter took the risk of naming the painter Guido Gonzato (1896–1955) as a referee. Schütter had read about Gonzato and knew that he lived in Chiasso, but they had never actually become acquainted. The border officers knew of Gonzato and contacted him accordingly. Although he was entirely clueless as to the identity of the man who had named him as a referee, Gonzato apparently grasped the nature of the situation and confirmed that Schütter should be allowed to enter Switzerland. The artists met not long afterwards, and a close friendship developed between them that continued between Schütter and Gonzato's family after the painter's death.

Schütter returned to Chur, but sought seclusion, and so rented a room in the hamlet of Churwalden, only a few miles to the south of his hometown. It was here, in the space of a fortnight, that he now composed

Guido Gonzato and family with Schütter, c. 1946

Guido Gonzato, Sera: *oil and tempera on board, 1943*

his First Suite for Clarinet and Piano. In 1995, Schütter wrote about it as follows:[3]

> This Suite is a kind of swansong to Europe as it faded away, the Old World. I specifically wanted to employ Romantic allusions because I thought we had no future. I adopted a nostalgic, late-Romantic, even Expressionistic tone, especially in the two homages it contains: in the 3rd movement, Lento, dedicated 'to Othmar Schoeck' – though I don't quote Schoeck here, I only endeavoured to employ similar harmonic means – and in the 4th movement, Allegro, 'to Igor Stravinsky', where I actually quote from his *Rite of Spring*. I dedicated the work as a whole to Werner Reinhart.[4]

This Suite also signified a close to an emotionally turbulent period in Schütter's life, with his months in Rome ushering in a period of intense reorientation.

---

[3] Published in the booklet text for the CD release *Meinrad Schütter: Kammermusik und instrumental begleitete Gesänge 1939–98*, Swisspan 510 316.
[4] Werner Reinhart (1884–1951), Winterthur industrialist and amateur clarinettist who was the most important patron of music and literature in Switzerland in the first half of the twentieth century, supporting composers as varied as Krenek, Schoeck, Stravinsky and Webern.

7

Military Service, *Medea* and Marriage

Schütter had no liking for anything military and was highly critical of everything to do with war. Being of an inventive nature, both in music and outside it, he now devised a plan to avoid being called up for service in the army. He had survived on little money in Rome, had returned to his native land in a semi-emaciated state, and now decided to stay awake throughout the night before his army medical examination and to drink a lot of coffee. He accordingly arrived at the army doctor's office the next morning pale, hollow-cheeked, sober and with a high pulse, and was promptly declared unfit for active duty. But Schütter also felt a sense of dutiful solidarity with his peers and was aware of the danger posed to Switzerland by the fascist regimes to the north and south. He therefore enlisted instead as a 'Hilfssoldat', an auxiliary soldier – which put him in the same category as many other Swiss artists and intellectuals at the time.

Schütter now entered the army after all. He was stationed in his home canton, first in the Sargans fortress and later in the region around Davos. In 1941 he was transferred to the frontier troops responsible for aerial observation at the San Bernardino Pass, near the border between Canton Graubünden and Italy. In his luggage he took a few clothes and a lot of music: scores, books and study materials, because he had just begun a composition course by correspondence with Willy Burkhard which he intended to pursue in his free hours at the top of the Pass.

Two years earlier, in November 1939, Burkhard had already advised Schütter 'to entrust himself to a capable teacher' in order to 'fill various gaps' in his musical knowledge, adding: 'For a while, you should even agree to undergo strict schoolmastering'.[1] Burkhard now took on this task himself. Schütter always held Burkhard in high esteem for the sensitive, friendly manner that he demonstrated in their correspondence and when correcting his assignments.

These lessons began in 1941 and lasted for two years. All that remains of Schütter's correspondence course today is ten letters, some of them incomplete, from which it emerges that Burkhard was dealing with a stubborn but willing pupil. Schütter found it difficult to subordinate himself

---

[1] Letter from Burkhard to Schütter, 7 November 1939.

Schütter in the Swiss Army, Sargans, c. 1940

to Burkhard's teaching methods and to the fixed rules of composition he
tried to impart, and he also tried to draw his teacher into discussions about
the methods he used – though Burkhard refused to engage with him on
this issue. Several years later, in a letter of 5 July 1947, Burkhard finally
confessed that he found it difficult to understand Schütter's music, which
he felt lacked any sense of synthesis and as a general rule was insufficiently
comprehensible.

At the San Bernardino, Schütter found himself immersed in a
magnificent primaeval landscape of craggy rock, barren scree and
snowfields, exposed to the elements. Inspired by the solitude and silence,
he now took up his Rome sketches for the opera *Medea* and resumed
work on it. Medea is a foreign 'other', an outcast who becomes both
victim and perpetrator. Schütter – stationed on an age-old crossing point
at Switzerland's southern border with fascist Italy – was undoubtedly
influenced in his choice of topic by the fatal dynamic of fear, insecurity,
betrayal and aggression from which fascism springs.

Reading Franz Grillparzer's great dramatic trilogy *The Golden Fleece*,
comprising *The Guest*, *The Argonauts* and *Medea*, gave him the final
impetus he required for his opera. Initially, Schütter planned a version
of the tale that adhered strictly to Grillparzer, though he subsequently
rejected it for being too 'belletristic'. As a writer whose origins lay in

the Enlightenment aesthetic of Goethe, Grillparzer seemed to Schütter to include too little of the mythological background of the principal character. He accordingly made a comparative study of the *Medea* plays by Grillparzer and Euripides, which helped him to recognise the grandeur of the topic and the possibilities inherent in it. The more he studied Euripides, the more Schütter felt able to go beyond Grillparzer's Classicism. Schütter had also come across a small volume in the Zurich Central Library containing the *Argonautica* by the Greek poet Apollonius Rhodius (c. 200BC) that featured the story of Medea and Jason, and which fascinated him with its stories of ancient Greek cults. Schütter ultimately decided to write a libretto that was a collage of his own, incorporating elements of the *Medea* story as told by Euripides, Grillparzer and Apollonius Rhodius (later, after the war, he would expand his text even further by drawing on Jean Anouilh, whose *Medea* of 1946 was given its first performance in German in 1948 in Hamburg).

Schütter worked intensively on *Medea* at the San Bernardino, even when he was supposed to be protecting the fatherland. One day, the officer on duty happened to be the Rumansh poet Andri Peer. He was making his rounds when he saw a dark, motionless figure at the top of the Pass. As he approached, he saw that it was someone shrouded in an oversized, thick loden cape with a hood. Peer went closer and lifted the cape, to find Schütter underneath, composing, with an electric torch for light. Being a poet himself, Peer refrained from taking disciplinary action, and recounted the tale gleefully after the War. Over fifty years later, Schütter composed one of his late song-cycles, the *Chanzuns da la not* ('Songs of the Night') to poems by Peer.

Before going to Rome, Schütter was already well-acquainted with Wagner's through-composed music dramas and his leitmotif technique. While in Italy, he also broadened his knowledge of Italian opera, studying its self-enclosed forms, the shape of the vocal lines and the manner of their accompaniment. In *Medea,* the initial version of which Schütter completed in 1941, the impact of his Italian experiences can be felt. It retains vestiges of traditional tonality, along with the forms of number opera. Schütter revised the work extensively over the ensuing eleven years, during which time he also incorporated elements of Schoenberg's twelve-note method. Although he avoided any strict application of dodecaphony, Schütter found that using tone-rows offered him a means of breaking away from what he called the 'seductiveness' of the Neo-Classical style that came so naturally to him.[2]

---

[2] Schütter in conversation in 2005.

Schütter in the Swiss Army, San Bernardino, 1942

Medea is a sorceress and the daughter of the King of Colchis on the Black Sea.[3] She helps Jason to win the Golden Fleece, then kills her father and brother before fleeing with Jason to Corinth and the court of Creon, where she subsequently bears Jason two sons. But the strangeness of her behaviour makes the Greeks shy away from her. Creon's daughter Creusa was the playmate of Jason's youth; they fall in love, and he ostracises Medea, a mere 'barbarian', who is now condemned to banishment, without her children. Jason's calculating pragmatism is contrasted with Medea's emotional unconditionality. Driven to desperation, Medea sets the palace on fire, kills Creusa and murders her two children. The opera ends with her inarticulate cry of absolute hopelessness.

Schütter wrote this opera without any commission or prospect of performance. Although he resisted any temptation to bring his Classical drama into the contemporary world, his opera was clearly born of a deep-seated need to express himself in an age of war and destruction, when people he knew were persecuted because of race or religion, and when the very collapse of European civilisation seemed imminent. His sympathies in the opera lie clearly with Medea herself.

Schütter also corresponded with Scherchen during his time on the San Bernardino, and told him about his work on *Medea*. In a letter of 5 September 1941, Scherchen wrote to Schütter: 'I am keenly awaiting the *Medea* fragments'. Schütter never sent them – which, given Scherchen's goodwill and his proven record of performing the music of his contemporaries, was tantamount to an act of self-harm on Schütter's part. But this shortsightedness was merely one of several occasions over the years when Schütter failed to respond to those who could have assisted him, which also helps to explain why his music was later ignored for so long.

Medea remained unpublished and unperformed. In the years that followed, Schütter sent the score of it to all manner of European opera houses in hopes that it might be 'discovered' by an intendant. Many claimed to be interested; Hans Rosbaud promised to help and even wanted to make suggestions for revising it – but he died shortly afterwards, in December 1962. When a friend much later asked Schütter what was happening with his *Medea*, he replied: 'I've laid it down, like an old wine'. It would take over half-a-century more before *Medea* was performed (and even then, only in a reduced concert version).

In 1943, Schütter married Claudia Mengelt, his close friend since their student days. She came from Ilanz, a tiny town in the Surselva region of Graubünden some fifteen miles west of Chur, and was born

---

[3] Colchis was located on the far-eastern shore of the Black Sea, incorporating the western-part of current-day Georgia, but also extending north-west to Tuapse and Sochi in Russia and south-west to Trabzon in Turkey.

into a Protestant family that adhered to the principles of the Evangelical theologian Leonhard Ragaz (1868–1945). When her impending marriage to the Catholic Meinrad Schütter was announced in 1943, it was apparently a shock to their acquaintances in Chur.[4] They were married on 11 September 1943 in an ecumenical ceremony – at the time still an unusual event in Switzerland – on the island of Rheinau in the Upper Rhine Valley, next to the German border. It was the wisest decision that Meinrad Schutter ever made. Oddly, it was also a decision his own father had foreseen. Before his death in 1935, Schütter Senior had spoken to Claudia of his worries that his son had chosen an uncertain profession, and had expressed his hopes that she might one day take care of him – Meinrad had himself remained oblivious of this conversation at the time.

Claudia Mengelt had been running a small leather workshop in the old town of Chur since the outbreak of war, and also gave singing and piano lessons to earn money. But in 1943 she was given a permanent job in the opera chorus of the Zurich City Theatre, and managed to wangle Meinrad a position there, too, as a freelance ballet répétiteur. Over the ensuing decades, it was Claudia who remained primarily responsible for giving their partnership a firm economic basis, and she always endeavoured to provide Meinrad with a home environment conducive to his being able to compose without external worries, shielding him as much as possible when the tribulations of everyday life threatened to overwhelm him. However, she was always adamant that no part of this arrangement constituted any 'sacrifice' on her part, but was a choice freely made. She was possessed of a sharp intellect, a sense of humour and charisma, and was quick-witted, too. She and Meinrad complemented each other perfectly. Their marriage, which remained childless, lasted until Claudia's death, 52 years later. Both remained at the Zurich Opera until their retirement. Meinrad understood how to make himself gradually indispensable there. Besides his duties as a répétiteur, he also worked behind the scenes as a lighting director – the man responsible for following the score offstage, ensuring that the instructions of the lighting designer were followed during performance. At his own request, he worked for several years at the Opera House without any permanent contract, though in his final decade there he took the advice of friends and got the House to issue him a standard contract. Claudia Schütter lost her singing voice early on as a result of the shock triggered by the unexpected suicide of her sister and was thereafter assigned the position of prompter – a job she loved and in which she excelled thanks to her presence of mind and multilingualism.

---

[4] Thus the recollection of Lucius Juon (1913–2015), an organist and choral conductor who lived in Chur at the time. *Cf.* also note 11 on p. 72, below.

*The Zurich Opera House in 1952, with the prompter's box
in the middle of the stage*

Numerous opera singers would insist on her being in the prompter's box during their performances, and she continued in the job well beyond retirement age.

Claudia thus disappeared into the prompter's box while her husband was free to roam behind stage, rummaging around in his free hours looking for interesting scores (and finding them, too). He thoroughly enjoyed his life in the twilight regions offstage where he could read and study unobserved, and benefitted from his unusual ability to withdraw into an inner world. Schütter was in general highly adept at avoiding anything that disturbed his sense of equanimity. He loved travelling and revelled in the anonymity of railway carriages, pubs and restaurants, claiming that one had to disappear 'from the danger zone of the piano' if one wanted to study scores properly. The piano, he claimed, was a place of real temptation for attempting the immediate realisation of one's compositional efforts, and he insisted that 'the only places where you can truly read and learn are railway cars, restaurants, or ships best of all, where you have no possibility of escape'.

The 1940s saw Schütter continue work on *Medea*; in 1943–44 he also composed the chorale *Ach, füll' unsere Seelen ganz* for mixed choir, and three songs variously in Graubünden dialect and in Rumansh that he wrote for the high-soprano voice of his wife: a *Bündner Scherzlied* ('Graubünden Joking Song'), *Das Langwieser Lied,* a setting of a folksong from the village of Langwies, and *Lamentatiun dal pulin, dall' ochetta e dal pulaster,* a 'lament of the young cockerel, the little goose and the fat hen' in face of their imminent demise for the Christmas feast – Schütter makes the most of the birds' onomatopoeic refrain of 'pul, pul, qua qua, curu, curu'. It is a setting of a folksong from the upper Engadine in the rarely spoken Rumansh dialect known as *putér,* though it probably originated in northern Italy and was brought to Graubünden with the many immigrants that arrived from Lombardy over the years. Schütter's last works of the decade were a setting of Goethe's *Wanderers Nachtlied* for men's chorus and orchestra in 1948 and *Et incarnatus est* for soprano, flute, oboe and string quintet in 1949, which was given its first performance by Radio Torino on 20 June 1949 under the direction of Mario Salerno.

8
Studies with Paul Hindemith, 1951–54

In 1950 Paul Hindemith was appointed the first professor at the Musicology Department of the University of Zurich. The Department had been founded several years earlier with two lecturers – Antoine Cherbuliez and Fritz Gysi – though neither was appointed a full professor. The Dean at the time, one Heinrich Straumann, initiated the debate about setting up a chair of musicology, and he found support in Emil Staiger, the best-known professor of German literature at the University, who declared himself in favour of inviting Hindemith to take up the post. Hindemith had already lived in Switzerland in the late 1930s, after the Nazi regime had compelled him to leave his post in Berlin. He then emigrated to the USA where he was appointed a professor at Yale University. After the War, Hindemith wanted to return to Europe. He saw Zurich as an ideal location, and so he accepted the invitation to teach there and gave his official, inaugural lecture at Zurich University on 24 November 1951.

Like many others of his generation, the isolation of the war years had left Schütter feeling a tremendous need to make up for the time and energies that had been lost. Although he was by now in his late 30s, he initially considered going to Ascona in Canton Ticino to study serial composition with Wladimir Vogel – the man responsible for teaching Schoenberg's method to Rolf Liebermann and many others among the early generation of Swiss serialists, and who in 1948 and 1949 co-organised the first-ever Twelve-Tone Congresses in Orselina and Milan respectively. But Schütter simply did not have the funds for either the tuition with Vogel or the living costs. Hindemith's move to Zurich offered Schütter the opportunity to study with an internationally known composer on his own doorstep. Schütter had long been fascinated by the clarity of structure and the transparency that he found in Hindemith's music and was especially fond of his early works such as the *Suite 1922* for piano and his one-act operas. Overall, he found Hindemith's ethical attitude in art and life congenial, and felt a kinship in his sense of humour, his irony and his antipathy towards the sentimental. Hindemith had already exerted a considerable influence on Schütter in his youth, and so when he was

Paul Hindemith with his class at Zurich University, c. 1954; from left:
Laurenz Custer, Werner Kaegi, Fritz Muggler, Schütter, Erwin R. Jacobi,
Hugo Käch, Rudolf Häusler, Heinz Lau, Hindemith, n.n.

appointed in Zurich, Schütter signed up for his lectures and seminars.[1]
This commitment occasioned a not inconsiderable financial outlay at a
time when Schütter's income was meagre, but the chance to learn from a
composer like Hindemith was one that Schütter could not let slip.

Hindemith's initial lectures dealt with 'Three-part writing' (the topic
that was to have been the third part of his *Craft of Musical Composition*,
but which was left unfinished at his death), then 'The nature of tonality' – a
topic that also occupied Schütter repeatedly throughout his life. According
to those who were present, Hindemith was a brilliant pedagogue, able to
make the complex comprehensible. Alfred Rubeli – who many years later
worked as an editor on Schott's 'Hindemith Complete Edition' – recalled
Hindemith in Zurich as follows: 'His outer appearance was already striking –
small in stature but with a pronounced head, with lively eyes, swift gestures
and a rapid manner of speaking in his Franconian accent – but the free,
unpretentious manner of how he lectured surprised us all the more'.[2]

[1] Schütter's fellow attendees at Hindemith's lectures included Willy Arnold, Hanny Bihr, Joseph Bihr, Laurenz Custer, Jürgen Henning, Eva Howe, Walter-Simon Huber, Erwin R. Jacobi, Werner Kaegi, Heinz Lau, Daniel Meier, Irene Meier, Fritz Muggler, Alfred Rubeli, Hans Schoop and Georges S. Tsouyopoulos.
[2] Alfred Rubeli, *Paul Hindemith und Zürich*, Hug, Zurich, 1969, p. 15.

But Schütter, too, left an impression on the others who were present. Werner Jöhl was a student of electrical engineering at ETH Zurich[3] at the time. He was also musically gifted, had already attended Cherbuliez's lectures in Zurich, and was allowed to register to hear Hindemith teach (Hindemith took a liking to him, too, and later invited him to visit his home in Blonay).[4] Jöhl later recalled how Schütter had stood out from the start:

> dressed in a double-breasted suit, he smoked, indulged in irony, hardly seemed to be present [...]. It was like he came from another world. He was self-confident and clearly believed in himself, for all his reticence. He seemed deliberately to close himself off, listening attentively without making any comment, and in the course of time assumed a kind of special position in the classes.

Schütter and Jöhl lost touch, but in 1992 they bumped into each other by chance on the Limmatquai, which runs along the east bank of the River Limmat in central Zurich, and thereafter they remained in frequent contact.

In later life, Schütter committed his own reminiscences of Hindemith to paper, which I here reproduce in full.

Meinrad Schütter: Notes on Paul Hindemith
(written in Küsnacht, 20 November 1995).

A lot has been written about Paul Hindemith that's both interesting and substantial. So I'd just like to add a few personal recollections. After having studied with Antoine Cherbuliez and at the Zurich Conservatoire, and after having absorbed the influences of Bartók, Stravinsky and Othmar Schoeck it seemed to me that studying with Hindemith would give me a link back to the polyphony of the Baroque.

In my great solitude while serving as a soldier in the war, I'd found enough time to work through Hindemith's *Craft of Musical Composition*. I also took a few correspondence lessons from Willy Burkhard. So I was not unprepared when I enrolled at the University of Zurich in 1951 and attended five [*recte*: four] semesters of lectures and seminars with Hindemith.

These lectures met with considerable interest – something that was still rather unusual in the field of musicology. It was his seminars that were especially important for me, for that was where we did practical work. You submitted your work and Hindemith corrected it - always calm,

---

[3] One of the foremost European institutions of tertiary education, ETH Zurich (the initials stand for *Eidgenössische Technische Hochschule*, 'Federal Institute of Technology') was founded by the Swiss federal government in 1854, with the stated mission of educating engineers and scientists; it still focuses primarily on science, technology, engineering and mathematics.

[4] Personal reminiscences of Werner Jöhl, told to the present writer.

objective, never pejorative nor in any dry, schoolmasterly manner, but with the humour that was characteristic of him and with an attentive interest in the music of his students.

For example, he spoke of how you shouldn't overstretch your material, expressing regret that a structural engineer would be sent to prison if he built a house that subsequently collapsed in on itself, whereas a composer would get off scot-free if he did something analogous in his music!

His curiosity and his emphasis on working directly with you gave the students the feeling that even their teacher himself was learning along with them. That's a sign of someone with a true pedagogical calling. I recall very well his outspoken vexation at the new ways in which Gregorian chant was beginning to be sung at that time, where its unique metrical freedom of breathing was being countered by an excessive rigidity of performance. It was in this context that he used the example of his *Mathis der Maler Symphony* to explain the conducting technique you could use to beat non-rhythmic unison passages in modern orchestral music.

It is well-known that Hindemith was particularly good at writing for brass instruments. It was the concerts of the regimental bands that came to Hanau, his birthplace, that were among his first significant impressions of music. He had also been a member of a military band when he was conscripted at an exceptionally young age.

One day, we were talking about the *Calvenmusik* [*recte: Calvenfeier*] by Otto Barblan.[5] I mentioned to him that the first performance in Chur in 1899 had been accompanied by the regimental band from Constance, which was famous at the time. Hindemith immediately knew the number of the regiment – which rather astonished me. He was able to mimic such brass instruments with his voice, especially the sharper pitch of French ensembles, while at the same time improvising marches on the piano. Such moments were hardly strictly musicological, but were unforgettably comedic.

Hindemith's remarks about his relationships with other composers and their music were revealing. He was friends with Stravinsky and reported on how Stravinsky had explained to him the libretto of his opera *The Rake's Progress* (1951). After a performance of the opera in Zurich,[6] the second production after its premiere in Venice, Hindemith reacted rather aloofly. He was also stand-offish about Gottfried von Einem's opera *Der Prozess* (after Kafka).[7] After the funeral service of Willy Burkhard [held in

---

[5] Barblan (1860–1943) was an organist and composer from Graubünden who studied in Chur, then at the Stuttgart Conservatoire and later taught organ and composition at the Geneva Conservatoire. His *Calvenfeier* of 1899 was a festival play with music commissioned to commemorate the Battle at Calven of 1499 between the Old Swiss Confederation and the Habsburg army of Maximilian I.

[6] The Zurich City Theatre gave the first-ever performance of *The Rake's Progress* in German translation on 3 November 1951, less than two months after the world premiere in Venice on 11 September.

[7] Schütter and Hindemith probably attended the guest performance given in the Zurich City Theatre on 1 February 1954 by the ensemble of the Bern City Theatre (which had given the Swiss premiere of

the Fraumünster in Zurich at 3 p.m. on 22 June 1955], who was known to have been an excellent teacher, we talked about compositional techniques and teaching methodologies – we were walking on the Bahnhofstrasse in Zurich – and I remarked that Schoenberg was said to have taught composition exercises in the style of Schumann.[8] Hindemith felt that this wasn't good, and was himself able to offer basic compositional techniques in all styles, even in extended tonality.

Time and again, I noticed how he grappled with the Schoenberg school, constantly searching for evidence to be able to argue against them – such as claiming that a listener is unable to distinguish between the principal and secondary voices ['Haupt- und Nebenstimmen']. A-cappella singing also presented insurmountable practical difficulties on account of the row technique. Here the concept of the 'social' came up. You can't abandon the listener to himself, said Hindemith!

During rehearsals for the second version of *Cardillac*,[9] which is no longer performed because people prefer the first version, I was working at the Opera House and was able to stand next to Hindemith and [Victor] Reinshagen,[10] the conductor, while they worked. During breaks in the rehearsals, I saw how Hindemith quickly tried to lighten up the orchestral writing in the sections adopted from the first version because they were too loud. In other words, he tried to reduce the volume, to give a 'facelift' to whole pages, as it were. Two or three years later, I found that selfsame score covered in dust under a cupboard in the City Theatre and recognised Hindemith's deletions in it. Today, that score is held by the Hindemith Institute in Frankfurt. Incidentally, Keilberth later made very similar deletions when he conducted *Cardillac* in Munich, without having known the [Zurich] score.

And I also recall what I saw at the stage premiere of [Schoenberg's] *Moses und Aron* in Zurich on 10 June 1957. After it ended, Hindemith stood in a corner for several minutes, deep in thought. In spite of his opinion that you couldn't make an opera out of that topic, he seemed deeply affected – which made an unforgettable impression on me. He must have recognised the greatness of this work, which no objections could possibly call into question.

---

the work in November 1953, only three months after the world premiere in Salzburg on 17 August).
[8] Schütter's source for this assertion is uncertain, though he could have heard it from the former students and colleagues of Schoenberg among his personal acquaintants, such as the conductor Hermann Scherchen or the composer-conductor Erich Schmid.
[9] Hindemith's revised version of *Cardillac* was given its world premiere at the Zurich City Theatre on 20 June 1952.
[10] The conductor Victor Reinshagen was born in Riga in 1908, went to school in Zurich, and studied there and in Berlin. From 1929 until his retirement he was a staff conductor at the Zurich City Theatre, where he conducted the Swiss premieres of Hindemith's revised *Cardillac*, Stravinsky's *The Rake's Progress*, Gershwin's *Porgy and Bess* and other works. He died in Zurich in 1992.

Schütter's work as a repetiteur at the Zurich City Theatre included playing for the Mario Volkart Dance School, which commissioned him to write a work for children in 1950. Schütter complied with a very funny chamber ballet for children – his second work for the stage after his opera *Medea*: *Dr Joggeli sött go Birli schüttle* ('Joggeli has to go and shake the pear tree'), composed in 1950–51 for eight dancers and two pianists after the picture book by Lisa Wenger; it was first performed in 1951 in a version for piano duet, played by Schütter and Alfred Zäch. Schütter rewrote the accompanying ensemble in 1986 for two pianos and percussion and added two movements to it, Introduzione and Passacaglia.

Lisa Wenger's picture book in Swiss dialect was first published in 1908 but remains one of the most popular children's books in Switzerland today. It's a cumulative tale (not unlike the English rhyme 'One man went to mow'). Here, the Master sends out Joggeli to shake the pear trees to harvest their fruit. But he's lazy, and instead lies down to sleep – as does everything else the Master sends out to prod Joggeli into working – a dog, a broom, a fire, a water bucket, but they're all just as lazy until the irate Master himself goes out at the end to get the job done. In his notes on the music, which follows Lisa Wenger's sequence of images, Schütter wrote: 'finally, the Master himself has to see to everything. Now everyone's actions begin to run in reverse, so the musical form also does the same (retrograde)'. Schütter had little experience of children, but skilfully adapted his music precisely to the imaginative world of his chosen audience – the fortunate choice of *Joggeli* as his topic also made the task easier for him.

Schütter composed several works during his studies with Hindemith. His *Triptychon for Soprano and Organ* of 1952 comprises two outer movements for organ enclosing a version for soprano and organ of his 1948 choral setting of Goethe's 'Wanderers Nachtlied'. The world premiere was sung by Schütter's wife, Claudia, in 1953, accompanied by Lucius Juon[11] on the organ. Also in 1953, Schütter turned again to choral composition with *Ögls e stailas* for men's chorus to a Rumansh text by Men Rauch and *Zuspruch II* for mixed chorus to a text by Nandor Währing; these were followed in 1954 by a further short piece for mixed chorus, *Hymnus: Tantum ergo* (Thomas Aquinus). Schütter rarely heard any of his

---

[11] Lucius Juon (1913–2015) was himself a figure of considerable importance in the Chur area. Born in Balgach, in the north-eastern corner of Switzerland, he studied with Hans Biedermann, Antoine-Élysée Cherbuliez and Paul Müller-Zürich, taking a post as organist in Arosa in 1937. In 1942 he was appointed organist and choir conductor of the Stadtkirche St Martin in Chur. Six years later he founded the Singschule in Chur and in 1958 the Kammerchor Chur, which he conducted until 1996; he also conducted the Collegium Musicum Chur and the Evangelische Bläservereinigung and was active as a composer. His programmes usually included works by contemporary composers, and in 1995, when Juon was in his early eighties, a local label released a CD of the Kammerchor Chur under his direction in a programme of music by Arvo Pärt.

A performance of Dr Joggeli sött go Birli schüttle *in Basel,*
25 January 2009

choral works performed, as they have long been deemed too difficult for
the amateur choirs that dominate the choral scene in Switzerland; of the
above three works, he only ever heard *Ögls e stailas,* at a concert given by
the Zurich Schubert Quartet in Basel in April 2005.

Schütter's biggest commission during the years of his study with
Hindemith was, however, not for a work of his own. In 1950, he had
sent a copy of his opera *Medea* to Hans Reinhart – writer, translator,
patron and wealthy joint heir of the Volkart company in Winterthur. A
correspondence between the two men ensued, and in 1951 Reinhart asked
Schütter, together with his friend and fellow Hindemith student Werner
Kaegi,[12] to arrange a performing version with piano of *Die Flüchtlinge*
('The Fugitives'), an opera in three acts by Alfred Schlenker to a libretto
by Hermann Hesse that the poet had written for him in 1910 (Hesse had
sketched several libretti at this time, though this is the only instance of
anyone actually setting one of them to music).[13] Schlenker (1876–1950)
was a dentist and amateur composer who had mixed with numerous artists
and had been responsible for introducing Othmar Schoeck to Hesse in
Gaienhofen in 1911. Schütter recalled in 1997 how his commission came
about:

[12] Werner Kaegi (1926–2024), Swiss composer, who later turned to electronic music and worked at
the Institute for Sonology at the University of Utrecht in Holland.
[13] Schlenker's original version of the opera is held today in his archives in the Zentralbibliothek
Zürich, shelfmark Mus NL 82 : I : B 1.

Schütter in 1955

Schlenker wrote the opera based on [...] a 'youthful indiscretion' of Hesse's that later became *Narziss and Goldmund*. Schlenker knew Hesse. They lived together in an artists' colony in Überlingen on Lake Constance. Schlenker was a dentist who worked for Prof. Binswanger [at his] psychiatric clinic for the mildly sick [the Sanatorium Bellevue in Kreuzlingen]; Nijinsky was also there [...].

With regard to this opera, Schoeck remarked that Hesse wouldn't like it! Schoeck also felt that the libretto was a sin of Hesse's youth. But I explained to him that the three of us [Reinhart, Kaegi and Schütter] had approached the matter quite cluelessly because it had been a commission from Reinhart. We didn't ask many questions. Schoeck liked the triumvirate solution with Kaegi [...]. Schlenker is said to have been an inspiring friend. He composed in his breaks at his dental practice, even also at night.

The piano reduction was completed in 1954 and sent to Heinrich Wollheim to make a fair copy.[14] On 16 October 1955, Reinhart wrote to Hermann Hesse as follows:

It is my great pleasure to be able to send you the vocal score of the *Flüchtlinge*, which has just been printed, in the hope that, once you've heard this beautiful work created by you and our dear friend, you will find it to have been arranged and completed to your satisfaction. Two very gifted composers who work at the Zurich City Theatre have completed this posthumous opera with reverence and deep empathy, and we hope to hear it in the foreseeable future, even if only with the soloists and a small chorus accompanied by the piano. My part in the work was restricted to editing the vocal parts, which I was largely able to undertake in the presence of the composer, to his fullest satisfaction.[15]

Apart from a run-through *chez* Reinhart in autumn 1955 to which the above letter implicitly refers, *Die Flüchtlinge* was never performed, and remains unstaged today. However, quite apart from the positive pecuniary aspect of the commission, it also had a delayed impact on Schütter himself, who later claimed that he had revisited the opera in the mid–1980s and that its lyrical, Romantic mood had inspired him while composing his Piano Concerto.

[14] Heinrich Wollheim (1892–1974) was a violist who was sent to Dachau by the Nazis on account of his having a Jewish father; Wilhelm Furtwängler intervened and engaged him as a copyist, which apparently saved Wollheim's life. After the war, Wollheim moved to Lake Constance and continued working as a copyist for Furtwängler and others.
[15] Schlenker had died in 1950, before Schütter began work on the vocal score.

9
In the Zurich Opera

Meinrad Schütter loved the theatre. In the thirty years that he worked at the Zurich City Theatre (today the 'Opera House'), from 1943 to 1973, he experienced it from all angles – backstage, front of stage, the entire inner organism of the immense system that is an opera house but that seems to dissolve into the background on the evening of a performance. He enjoyed a relationship of mutual esteem with the conductor Nello Santi, who for many years was its Music Director, and he also experienced a myriad of conductors, directors, composers and world-renowned soloists. He worked closely as a repetiteur with many of them, knowing all their moods (it seems that only Rudolf Nureyev proved truculent enough to rob Schütter of his otherwise inexhaustible sense of humour). It was also primarily as a repetiteur that Schütter was known to all and sundry at the opera house. In a review of two albums of his works in *Tempo* in 2001, Peter Palmer wrote: 'As a student in the late 1960s, I met Schütter when he was on the staff of the Zurich Opera. I knew that he wrote music, but nobody at that time – and least of all the man himself – suggested that here was a creative artist of stature'.[1]

In later life, Schütter would recount with glee the tales of the world premieres that he had experienced there, from Schoenberg to Hindemith, though with a tendency to meander down anecdotal labyrinths in the course of the telling. However, by the time I was able to discuss Schütter's career with him, much had already fallen into oblivion, with our conversations focusing primarily on Schütter's own music.

Schütter was deeply impressed by the personality of the conductor Carlos Kleiber (1930–2004), who seemed devoted to his art with every fibre of his being. He was the son of the conductor Erich Kleiber, was considered unpredictable and highly sensitive, and preferred to avoid the public eye. Many called the younger Kleiber an eccentric, but Schütter would have none of it. He once described an unusual rehearsal with Kleiber alone at the piano over a lunchbreak. They went through the work to be performed, with Kleiber as approachable as a child, explaining, discussing

---

[1] Peter Palmer, untitled review of assorted CDs of Swiss music, *Tempo*, No. 218 (October 2001), pp. 56–58, here p. 56.

Rehearsals in Zurich for Rolf Liebermann's Penelope in 1954.
Hans Rosbaud conducts, Claudia Schütter is seated at the front

and singing the work until he was ultimately lying under the grand piano, from where he continued to conduct.

Schütter's work at the Zurich Opera House kept him very busy, but to supplement his income he also took on the directorship of small amateur choirs and worked as a church organist. His choir work usually ended after a relatively brief period at his own request, since he was always keen to include contemporary music in his programmes but was also not overly talented as a pedagogue (despite having studied at teachers' training college). As a result, he soon overtaxed his singers, who in turn lost interest. He once even nicknamed himself the 'choir liquidator', since his efforts on one occasion had ended when the choir he was supposed to conduct disintegrated completely.

In 1966, Schütter's mother, Emilie, died. She had found it difficult to have any kind of relationship with Meinrad, in contrast to her favoured, second son, Pepi. Looking back in May 2001, Schütter recalled: 'Basically, my mother possessed artistic talent but was incapable of relationships – you might even say: almost cold'. She sang and was apparently very musical – talents that Schütter clearly inherited – but she never attended any of his concerts and was if anything ashamed of his musical language, which she found strange. Although they never really got along, Meinrad and

Franz Rederer: portrait of Meinard Schütter, dated 16 March 1956.
Black and red chalk with ink

Claudia always did their best to ensure that she was looked after. Schütter never dedicated a piece to his mother – which was unusual for him, because most of his works have dedicatees. However, the manuscripts in his archives do include a single, undated sheet on which he had at some point begun a composition for cello and chamber orchestra entitled *Geburtstags-Elegie für Mama* ('Birthday Elegy for Mum'). Not only is it unfinished; it was never even really begun, as if in itself an indication of a helplessness that lacked any means of expression. Fifty years later, this unresolved relationship with his mother, which was overlaid with feelings of guilt, would overshadow Schütter's final weeks, tormenting him with nightmares and visions of dread.

These years when Schütter's focus was at the Opera House were not conducive to his work as a composer. Where the song with piano accompaniment had been a prime focus in his earlier years, he wrote only four in the 1950s and 1960s – *Matg* ('May'; Gian Caduff) in 1955, *Der Tod* ('Death'; Matthias Claudius) in 1956, *Sehnsucht* ('Yearning'; Gebhard Karst) in 1960 and *Pos o Matg* ('May you, o May'; Caduff) in 1962. Gebhard Karst was a cousin of Schütter's who had gone blind at the age of sixteen, later became a successful businessman, helped to set up a school for the blind in Canton Zug (the Sonnenberg) and also wrote poetry throughout his life. Two orchestral works were the only larger-scale pieces to be written in these years: a *Suite for Small Orchestra* in 1955, which was given its first performance in 1960 in Chur by the Winterthur City Orchestra under Ernst Schweri Jr, and the *Duo Concertante 'Quasi una fantasia'* for violin, viola and orchestra of 1966, which was first performed by the Symphony Orchestra of Lake Constance in Winterthur on 2 April 1967. It was dedicated to Ernst Schweri Sr, who had died early that year, and is based on the Bach chorale 'Ach, wie flüchtig, ach, wie nichtig ist des Menschen Leben' ('Oh, how fleeting and insubstantial is the life of man'). The main newspapers seem not to have bothered sending any reviewers; the critic of *Der Freie Rätier* from Canton Graubünden could not help mentioning how Schütter supposedly 'piled up daring sounds', but nevertheless deemed the *Duo Concertante* a work 'of unusual expressive power' that was an 'honourable monument' to the deceased Ernst Schweri.[2]

These years might have been somewhat fallow in compositional terms, but they did bring initial public honours for Schütter, including a prize from the Eos Foundation in Zurich in 1967 and a 'recognition prize' from the Cultural Commission of the Canton of Graubünden in 1970. In 1976, Meinrad and Claudia gave up their apartment in the city of Zurich and moved to the Seestrasse in Küsnacht, only five miles away on the eastern

---

[2] 'hr' in *Der Freie Rätier*, 12 April 1967.

Claudia and Meinrad Schütter, New Year's Eve 1961, on the opening night of a production of Johann Strauss' Die Fledermaus *at the Zurich Opera*

banks of Lake Zurich. From there, it was only a few steps to the lakeside promenade. Their new apartment was sunny and exuded an old-fashioned, Biedermeier cosiness that seemed strangely out of synch with Schütter's personality. It was also noisy, however, on account of non-stop passing traffic. Küsnacht was becoming a haven for local millionaires, and Meinrad used to refer mockingly to his new abode as situated in the 'slums' of the Gold Coast (as the area was nicknamed). They had a small back-garden with a beautiful apple tree that Claudia Schütter loved throughout the year, whether in spring when it blossomed or when it bore fruit in the autumn, which she picked tirelessly and cooked in all manner of ways. For weeks on end afterwards, visitors would be entertained with copious amounts of delicious apple compote.

It was in the year of their move, 1976, that Meinrad Schütter retired. Claudia, too, increasingly turned down requests to prompt at the Opera House. Instead, Meinrad now took on the position of organist at the Catholic Church in Zollikon, the small town that lies between Küsnacht and the city of Zurich proper. He played the organ there for the next 30 years, until only a few months before his death, making both friends and 'enemies', as he did not refrain from exposing the congregation to the sounds of the new, often offering long improvisations at the close of a Mass that prompted many a churchgoer to a rapid exit. As a devout but critical Catholic, Schütter loved to talk with the clergy – his favourites in

Claudia Schütter in the prompter's box in the Zurich Opera House, c. 1970

Zollikon were Fathers Joseph Mächler and Karl Weber, whom he found open and enlightened in their views – though the priests of the parish naturally came and went. These friendships by no means made Schütter any more conscientious about practising than was his wont. Once, during

Küsnacht, as seen from Lake Zurich in 2012

Schütter in the 1960s

Father Karl Weber and Schütter in 2000

a telephone call in 2004, he said: 'I have to play in church, it's an organ piece by someone else. But I'll tear it up tonight and put it back together in a different order'.

10
Friends and Colleagues

Meinrad Schütter led a relatively secluded, unspectacular life, content with himself and his world. He did not often feel any need to leave his immediate environment, but when he did, he was highly communicative, and his circle of friends and acquaintances included poets, musicians, authors, painters and other artists, some of whom became lifelong friends. In several cases, his friends also provided texts for his songs and choral works.

The Conti Restaurant behind the Zurich Opera House had long been a popular haunt for its personnel, and for a 'Conti Circle' that used to meet there regularly. This Circle included the writers Walter Mehring, Rudolf Humm, Pierre Walter Müller and Max Mumenthaler, the translator Elke Gilbert, the painters Adolf Herbst and Max Hunziker, the art-historian Fritz Hermann, and others who came and went. Claudia and Meinrad Schütter were permanent fixtures in the Conti Circle, with Meinrad using the breaks between the acts to call in and see who was there. It was also his custom after a performance to drink a last glass of wine among discussion-hungry friends.

Walter Mehring (1896–1981) seems not to have played an active role in the Conti Circle, preferring to sit at the end of the table, listening more than speaking. He was born in Berlin, joined the Expressionists there, helped to set up a local Dada association, and made a name for himself through the texts he wrote for the Berlin cabaret 'Schall und Rauch' in the early days of the Weimar Republic. He was left-wing and Jewish and had to flee Germany in 1938 to avoid incarceration, subsequently escaping to the USA in 1941 via Switzerland and a French internment camp. He returned to Europe after the war and lived quietly in Zurich, often on the breadline, his achievements largely ignored by local officialdom. 'His was a fragile nature', remarked Meinrad Schütter. 'Sensitive, with great charisma, impressive mental acuity and possessed of a sense of irony in both his verse and his prose.' Mehring also already knew Elke Gilbert from the time when they were both in New York exile from the Nazis – though as Schütter recalled, an odd coolness always obtained between the two of them. Schütter set three Mehring poems from his *Transatlantic Psalter* to music (two songs for voice and piano: *Denn: Aller Anfang ist schwer* ('For:

The Conti Restaurant behind the Zurich Opera House, 1972

All Beginnings are Difficult') in 1980 and *Plainte et compleinte d'un pauv' vieux chien* ('The Complaint of a Poor Old Dog') in 1985, revised in 1996, and the male-voice chorus *Eines Strolches Trostlied* ('A Vagabond's Song of Comfort') in 1993).

The painter Adolf Herbst (1909–83) was an introverted, unconventional thinker who, like Schütter, charted an unconventional path through life and endured similar privations on account of it. Schütter visited him regularly in his studio on the Neumarkt in the centre of Zurich. Their extant correspondence reveals him to have been an inspired, humorous letter-writer who often included marginal drawings or collages when he wrote. Max Hunziker (1901–76) was a painter, book-illustrator, graphic artist and a master of stained-glass windows (it was for the last of these that he became especially well-known in Switzerland). He was a close friend of the art-historian Fritz Hermann (1922–2008), who was also a regular in the Conti Circle and who lived in Küsnacht, close to the Schütters. It was

Walter Mehring in the Hotel Opera in Zurich, 1976

Hermann who gave Schütter his last-ever commission – for a Quartet for Oboe, Trumpet, Bassoon and Cello in 2005.

Over the years, the Conti Circle dissipated, and its remaining members – still including Claudia and Meinrad Schütter – began meeting instead in the 'Steinburg' in Küsnacht. They were joined by Gian Nogler (later the Zurich University Archivist), and occasionally by the sculptors Eduard Spörri (1901–95) and Hildi Hess (1911–98).

Schütter's artist friends also included a painter from Sumatra by the name of Saudara Salim (1908–?), who called himself 'Salim' for short. He had studied with Fernand Léger in Paris in the 1930s and wrote in Dutch and French; two catalogues from Amsterdam and Paris, plus a review of an exhibition in Sète in 1950, have survived in Schütter's archives. Schütter often spoke of Salim, and owned several large, abstract oils and watercolours, several of which he still hung on his wall after he moved into a small apartment in a retirement home in Küsnacht towards the close of his life. All other traces of Salim seem to be lost.

Schütter also maintained another, less work-centred circle of friends and acquaintances, several of them from his native canton of Graubünden, including the artists Leonhard Meisser (1902–77), Otto Braschler (1909–85) and Verena Zinsli (1923–2019), the musician Willy Byland from Chur (1912–75), the sculptor Ludwig Stocker from Basel (b. 1932) and the writers Paolo Gir from S-chanf in Graubünden (1918–2013) and

The painter Adolf Herbst in 1975

Albert Vigoleis Thelen (1903–89), who was originally from Germany. Thelen was a gifted storyteller[1] who shared Schütter's tendency to use irony to play down the uncomfortable aspects of life (including politics). Schütter set two of Thelen's poems to music: 'Nächtliche Lampe' ('Night Lamp') for voice and piano in 1980 and 'Porcorum causa' ('For the Sake of Pigs') for speaker and piano in 1982 – the latter an anti-fascist exercise in sarcasm. The two men did not meet often, but their fondness for tilting at metaphorical windmills ensured a distinct sense of kinship.

These circles of Schütter's friends are notable in that they comprised mostly painters and writers. Schütter never collected art *per se* – as he once remarked, he lacked not just the necessary money and time but also the impulse to collect. But he was a keen observer of the visual arts, and both he and Claudia were the regular recipients and dedicatees of paintings and drawings, just as Schütter delighted in dedicating works of music to his friends. His distinctive profile also inspired assorted artists to paint, draw or sculpt him, from the Viennese artist Franz Rederer (whose portrait of Alban Berg is famous for long gracing the Philharmonia scores of his works) to Otto Braschler, Fritz Hug, Verena Zinsli and Ludwig Stocker, resulting in a notable collection of Schütter portraits over the years.

---

[1] Lothar Schröder, *Vigoleis – ein Wiedergänger Don Quijotes: Eine Untersuchung zum literarischen Lebensweg des Helden im Prosawerk Albert Vigoleis Thelens*, Grupello Verlag, Düsseldorf, 2007.

Schütter's friendship with the Italian artist Guido Gonzato (1896–1955) had begun during his military service on the Bernardino Pass.[2] He became one of Schütter's closest friends, though his early death meant they knew each other for barely more than a decade. His family originally came from Colognola al Colli in the province of Verona, and had moved to Chiasso in Switzerland in 1913. After the Second World War, Gonzato, his wife and their three children moved to nearby Mendrisio. Stylistically, Gonzato was close to Italian Expressionism, and he found it difficult to sell his works in Switzerland in the 1940s. Schütter accordingly stepped in to act on occasion as his 'art dealer', helping Gonzato to sell paintings so that he could at least feed his family. Schütter was no businessman, but possessed the necessary eloquence and self-confident manner to be able to convince those with money of the logic and benefit of parting with it to purchase a painting. He used to recall with delight how he had once managed to convince the wife of a wealthy factory-owner in Canton Glarus to buy a Gonzato. She walked through the house with Schütter to find a suitable piece of wall to hang it, but her walls were already full. She finally opened the door to her bedroom, strode over to a female nude in an imposing landscape that hung over the marital bed, took it determinedly down from the wall, hung her chosen Gonzato in its place, and commented drily: 'Basta la nuda!'.

Schütter's friendship with the artist Verena Zinsli was one shared by both their spouses. In the early 1960s, Verena Zinsli and her husband Philipp (1919–95), a medical doctor and an amateur connoisseur of music, established a home in Lürlibad on the outskirts of Chur as a centre of culture after the fashion of the early twentieth-century salons of the bigger German-speaking cities. Their newly built house was notable for its open, modern architecture, and ideal for holding house concerts at regular intervals. Philipp Zinsli loved Mozart especially, but was also open to everything new. Meinrad had known Philipp Zinsli while still at school, and when their spouses also became acquainted, the two couples together established a firm friendship that lasted for the rest of their lives. Schütter attended all their house concerts, and they in turn frequently organised world premieres of his works. One such occasion was the first performance of Schütter's Clarinet Trio in 1993 (a work dedicated to Philipp Zinsli and given a fine interpretation by the Calamus Trio, comprising Josias Just, Martin Zimmermann and Martin Imfeld). The conductor Räto Tschupp was among those present – he knew Schütter well, and besides being a fellow native of Chur, he had also conducted several of his works in the early 1980s. Tschupp urged Schütter – not for the first time – 'finally'

---

[2] Discussed on p. 56, above.

Philipp and Verena Zinsli, c. 1990

to put together a catalogue of his works, as that could help to promote them and facilitate their performance. Schütter was never going to invest the time and energy necessary, and so instead passed on the task to me. This book is thus a late consequence of the discussions held on that evening in Chur in 1993, as was the establishment of a Meinrad Schütter Society in 2002, dedicated to the promotion of his music.

The Zinslis engaged well-known musicians from Zurich and Chur for concerts, sometimes even from abroad. The standards at these house concerts were high enough for the press to take notice sometimes, too. When the Zinslis hosted several world premieres by Schütter at a concert in November 1978, one Heinrich Jecklin wrote a review for the main regional newspaper, the *Bündner Zeitung*, which was published on 23 November under the title 'Very interesting house concert'. He wrote oddly of Schütter's 'radical need for expression that knows no banality', though also of his 'memorable originality'. This reaction confirms one of the notable aspects of the reigning aesthetic at the Zinslis' house concerts: they provided a venue for contemporary music that many in the provinces found uncomfortable to hear, though gently and cleverly 'packaged' alongside more familiar fare. Hearing a work for the first time is a significant moment for any composer; the Zinslis made this possible with first-rate performers in a convivial, amicable setting.

Two thick guestbooks – today almost falling apart at the seams –
testify to the events *chez* Zinsli and to their attendees. They include the
concert programmes and the comments of the participants, inevitably in
high spirits after the event – including musicians such as Räto Tschupp
(together with his wife, the architect Els Tschupp), the pianists Warren
Thew and Sara Novikoff, writers such as Vigoleis Thelen and Gian
Caduff, and local patrons such as Ruth and Roman Barandun. One of
the last large-scale concerts *chez* Zinsli was held on 18 September 1993
to celebrate Claudia Schütter's 85th birthday, the musicians comprising
Stefania Huonder (mezzo-soprano), Elisabeth Thurnherr (violin), René
Oswald (clarinet) and myself on piano, in a programme comprising
Janáček, Shostakovich and Schütter. There were three first performances
of works by Schütter, the main work being his tone poem for piano about
the local legends of hauntings at the Scaläratobel ravine, *Churer Legende
von Spukgeistern und Spiegeleien* (1988), dedicated to Verena Zinsli (one
of many works dedicated to her or her husband). Verena Zinsli often drew
Schütter's portrait, documenting him over the years right up until the last
months of his life.

In 2011, five years after Schütter's death, the Graubünden writer Oskar
Peer published his reminiscences of a Zinsli house concert:

> One man who was a regular guest here with his wife remains unforgettable
> for everyone – the musician and composer Meinrad Schütter. I have
> rarely known such a witty, entertaining human being – and one who was
> also kind and imaginative. He was blessed, as it were: someone who had
> managed to retain something of a child's paradise inside him. You saw it
> in his face, and you could hear it in his voice. When he recounted some
> reminiscence or other from his schooldays, or from his military service,
> it was exciting and amusing – not really because of the story itself, but
> because of its narrator. He would sing some forgotten cantonal school
> song from Chur, then he stood up to demonstrate with arms and legs how
> certain female opera singers would scuttle across the stage, and on one
> occasion he played at the grand piano, accompanying someone who was
> singing one of his idiosyncratic, enigmatic compositions.[3]

It was *chez* Zinsli that Ruth and Roman Barandun first met Meinrad and
Claudia Schütter. Ruth Barandun began championing Schütter's music in
the early 1980s at a time when it was rarely performed, if at all. She later
recalled:

> Over the years, two folders filled up with letters of recommendation and
> samples of his music that I sent to conductors and concert promoters all

---

[3] Oscar Peer, 'Erinnerungen an den Schützenweg 15 in Chur', in *Bündner Jahrbuch: Zeitschrift für
Kunst, Kultur und Geschichte*, No. 53 (2011), p. 166.

Verena Zinsli: Meinrad Schütter at the piano, c. 1990

around the world. It was hardly encouraging to get so many refusals and empty promises, but it was all the more gratifying when we occasionally enjoyed a success![4]

And there were indeed successes. Ruth Barandun organised a concert for Schutter's 70th birthday at the Chur City Theatre in 1981 with Karin Ott (soprano) accompanied by the Camerata Zürich under the baton of Räto Tschupp. It was also thanks to the financial assistance of Ruth Barandun that Schütter was able to hear the first performance of his *Serenade for Voice and String Trio* in the Chur Town Hall on 31 January 1986, over 50 years after he had composed it. It was sung by Helen Keller (soprano) and accompanied by the Munich String Trio (Ana Chumachenko, Oscar Lysi and Wolfgang Mehlhorn). The same musicians also released the *Serenade*

---

[4] Communication with the author.

on an LP entitled *Bündner Komponisten* ('Composers from Graubünden')
featuring works by Paul Juon, Otto Barblan and others.[5]

The third and final group of friends that was vital to Meinrad Schütter
was in the Schlaraffia fraternity. This association was founded in Prague
in 1859 as a kind of humorous pendant to the Freemasons; its goals are to
promote music and the arts among its members and to uphold tolerance
and friendship. Its members are always men, and it is mostly found in
the German-speaking world and in the USA (it was banned by the Nazis
and, after the Second World War, by the communists in eastern Europe).
Schütter joined on the initiative of his wife, who thought it would do her
rather introverted husband good to join a society whose members had
an attitude to life not dissimilar to his own. He took real delight in the
absurdities the Schlaraffia offered, and his brethren loved his sense of
fun and his witty, polemical pronouncements. He established long-lasting
friendships through the fraternity, such as with the singer Rolf Kaltenbach
and the cellist Jarmo Vainio, but he also found the atmosphere there to
be ideal for testing the waters with new music as he composed it. The
Schlaraffia enabled him to live out his childlike delight in musical sketches
and improvised musical games in the oddest of instrumental combinations,
oscillating between profundity and absurdity – and his efforts found a
willing audience. The works he composed for the Schlaraffia also included
'serious' essays, however, such as his *Fanfares* for wind instruments of 2004.

This account leaves only the tale of how I got to know the Schütters.
It began as an encounter between our dogs one hot July day in 1972 on
the Rhine bridge in Splügen – a very beautiful, old village on the San
Bernardino Pass. Our family was returning home, exhausted, from a
daytrip to the high-lying Suretta Lakes. We walked in single file, father
and mother in front, then our tired dachshund trotting along the pass,
followed by our two young daughters (six and seven years old) some way
behind. Some distance away, there stood a gentleman with a hat on his
head that was somewhat too small for him; a woman who was obviously
his wife sat on the wall of the bridge next to him, a flower behind her ear.
They watched our procession with obvious amusement – in retrospect, our
situation must have exuded a certain comedy. They had a black poodle
with them.

Then our dogs discovered each other, and the scene came suddenly to
life. Poodle and dachshund raced around our legs, wagging their tails at
a hellish speed. Schütter stood up and came slowly towards us, uttering
witticisms that I cannot now remember but that resulted in laughter on
all sides. We were still together that same evening and had our first glass

---

[5] Ex Libris EL 16 994, Zurich, 1987.

of wine together in the Hôtel Bodenhaus in Splügen. It was then that we discovered we had more in common than pet dogs, for music was our prime interest.

What began as a casual friendship turned into mutual visits and holidays spent together, and then turned into a real collaboration when we were joined by Stefania Huonder, a contralto from Schütter's home canton. He was fascinated by the deep, warm timbre of her voice. It was Schütter who brought us together for our first recital, in Basel in 1989, which was followed by many more. We became a regular duo and gave concerts in Switzerland and abroad. Schütter began to write songs and piano works for us – of which perhaps his Rumansh-language cycle *Chanzuns da la not* ('Songs of the Night'), composed in 1994 to poems by his friend Andri Peer, is worthy of special mention. Schütter often joined us on our concert travels, as we made sure that we included his songs on our programmes whenever possible. We also gave regular, private house-concerts on the Multenweg in Basel, often as dress rehearsals for our public concerts, and Schütter – with his unerring, theatrical wit – soon became the focus of a circle of friends, music-lovers and supporters who remained committed to his music over the last twenty years of his life and beyond. His songs were of such high quality that I arranged for the Swiss music publishing house Nepomuk (run by the composer-pianist Francis Schneider) to publish 25 of them in several volumes over the next few years, along with a selection of his chamber music. His finest songs have meanwhile also been released on compact disc, recorded by Stefanie Huonder, Karin Ott and others.[6]

---

[6] For example, *Meinrad Schütter – Lieder (1931–1994)*, with Karin Ott, Janka Wyttenbach, Stefania Huonder, Ute Stoecklin and Otto Georg Linsi, on Uranus 602 (1997) and *Duo en treis*, with Stefania Huonder and Ute Stoecklin, on CD Swisspan SP 51723 (2006).

11
The Piano Concerto

On 25 January 1981, Schütter's *Grosse Messe* was given its first-ever performance in full. Three movements – the Sanctus, Benedictus and Agnus Dei – had been heard in November 1975 by the Chur Chamber Choir under Lucius Juon, and had elicited the praise of the critic of the *Neue Zürcher Zeitung* for their 'highly personal' style.[1] The same critic, Martin Ruhoff, was even more impressed when he heard the whole work with the same performers, a little over five years later:

> We heard a work of great craftsmanship and significant density of expression […]. The most beautiful sections of the work undoubtedly include the ingenious Hosanna fugue and the Benedictus, which is constructed as a passacaglia (with a great sense of climax) […]. [This was] an impressively unified, coherent performance of this highly demanding work.[2]

The organist on the evening received especial praise: it was the composer and keyboard player Martin Derungs (1943–2023), who later recalled how his initial impression ('The music is unwieldy, with ever new ideas alternating seemingly without any logic') was replaced by its opposite during rehearsals ('every gesture does find its meaning').[3]

The second major event of the year 1981 for Schütter was a concert held in Chur on 5 May, when Räto Tschupp conducted the Camerata Zürich in several of his orchestral songs and Kreusa's aria from *Medea*, with the soprano Karin Ott as soloist – fresh from her recent success as the Queen of the Night for Herbert von Karajan's *Zauberflöte* recording with the Berlin Philharmonic, and about to be given a contract at the Vienna State Opera. The main Swiss newspapers failed to send their critics – hardly unusual for a concert two hours from the metropolis of Zurich – but a radio recording survives that makes one wish to hear the rest of the opera.

---

[1] Martin Ruhoff ('mr'), 'Kammerchor Chur', *Neue Zürcher Zeitung*, Vol. 196, No. 280, 2 December 1975.

[2] Martin Ruhoff ('mr'), 'Uraufführung einer Messe', *Neue Zürcher Zeitung*, Vol. 202, No. 22, 28 January 1981.

[3] Martin Derungs, 'Begegnung mit Meinrad Schütter', in Stoecklin, *Meinrad Schütter 1910–2006*, p. 169.

This increasing attention spurred Schütter on to further compositional activity – he was now just over 70 years of age – and after Tschupp and Ott, other prominent Swiss musicians also began to engage with his music, such as the young clarinettist René Oswald, for whom Schütter wrote *Four Pieces for Solo Clarinet* in 1982–83 (first performed in their first version in Lenzerheide on 17 March 1983), a largely serial work. Oswald also performed regularly as a duo with the pianist Annette Weisbrod in the 1980s, and it was for them that Schütter wrote his Second Suite for Clarinet and Piano in 1984. Both these works were dedicated to Oswald, who continued to collaborate with Schütter in the years that followed, when he was appointed the artistic director of the International Summer Festival in the picturesque village of Obersaxen (Canton Graubünden). This was a course organised specifically for wind-players, and for which Oswald engaged prominent artists such as André Jaunet (flute), Burckhard Glaetzner (oboe), Michael Höltzel (horn) and Günter Pfitzenmeier (bassoon). Besides master-classes, the Festival also featured concerts by the participants and the tutors. Schütter wrote his *Ricercare* for oboe, clarinet, horn and bassoon for the 1983 Festival, and the same concert saw the premiere of his *Serenade* for flute, oboe and clarinet of 1934. Schütter's most substantial chamber work was also written for the Obersaxen Festival: the Wind Octet for flute, oboe, three clarinets, two bassoons and horn, performed there in 1985. A further sign of Schütter's increasing status was a concert organised in his home city of Chur that year to celebrate his 75th birthday – admittedly half a year early, held on 22 March 1985, and in fact a joint event also intended to commemorate the 50th birthday of his fellow Graubünden native, the composer Gion Antonio Derungs (1935–2012).[4] Claudia Schütter loved birthdays, and while Meinrad tended to forget those of others, he had no objection to being fêted himself. All the same, he could not resist an act of subversion on this occasion, for which he wrote a *Medicinal Cantata* for voice, speaker, flute, piano and harpsichord to a text of his own. In private, Schütter always referred to it as the *Prostate Cantata*. It was a reworking of an autobiographical occurrence involving a medical misdiagnosis, and depicted with satirical exaggeration all the possible ramifications for the male anatomy of the heavy doses of oestrogen that constituted the preferred therapy at that time. Schütter dedicated the work to his friend Philipp Zinsli, who as a medical doctor had realised the error of the diagnosis in Schütter's case and had promptly advised the cessation of treatment. Schütter assumed the piano part for the first performance. Opinion was divided about it – some found it delightfully witty, while

---

[4] 'Derungs' is a not uncommon surname in Graubünden; Gion Antonio and the previously mentioned Martin Derungs were not directly related to each other.

others found it juvenile and inappropriate for an occasion intended by the high society of Chur as a serious commemoration of their two leading composers. Claudia Schütter was deeply embarrassed, spent the weeks before the concert in dread of it, and admitted that 'I wished the ground could have swallowed me up'.[5]

The year 1985 was Schütter's most productive to date. Besides the Wind Octet and *Medicinal Cantata*, much of the year was taken up by a piano concerto – the only work of its kind that Schütter ever composed, despite being a pianist himself. Its origins lay in a concert that Schütter had attended three years previously, in February 1982, when he had heard the young pianist Tomás Kramreiter in a recital at the Zurich Tonhalle. Kramreiter was the son of a Viennese church architect who had managed to emigrate to Madrid in 1940, returning home with his family only in 1950. Kramreiter studied at the Mozarteum in Salzburg and with Nadia Boulanger in Paris before embarking on a successful career as a concert pianist. Schütter was immediately enthused by his playing and decided he had to write a piece for him: it became the *Variations on a Rhythm*, to which Schütter gave a subsidiary title taken from Messiaen's *Technique of my Musical Language*, namely: 'With very inexact augmentations or diminutions, one arrives at making rhythmic variants rather than augmentations or diminutions properly so called'.[6] Kramreiter as yet knew nothing of the piece that he had inspired. But after he and his wife Virginia moved to Switzerland in the autumn of 1982, she became acquainted with Schütter during a chamber-music evening at which she played, organised by the Schlaraffia. She thereupon introduced him to her husband, and the immediate result was a private concert that Kramreiter gave at the Zurich house of a music-loving doctor by the name of Walter Hitzig, featuring the first private performance of Schütter's new Variations; he gave its public premiere shortly afterwards, on 26 January 1983 at a recital in the main hall of the Zurich Conservatoire.

Schütter's friendship with Kramreiter had been determined in part by chance meetings, and a similar serendipity was now the catalyst for another work for the same man. It was at about this time that Ruth Barandun sent a score of Schütter's *Duo Concertante* for violin, viola and orchestra of 1966 to Yehudi Menuhin in hopes that he might play it. He didn't, but sent it instead to his colleague Edmond de Stoutz, the conductor of the Zurich Chamber Orchestra, suggesting that it was worthy of putting on his programme. De Stoutz didn't perform it either, but a recommendation from Menuhin was enough to make him take notice of the composer.

---

[5] In conversation with the author.
[6] Olivier Messiaen, trans. John Satterfield, *The Technique of my Musical Language*, Vol. 1, Alphonse Leduc, Paris, 1956, p. 19.

Kramreiter recalls de Stoutz as commenting: 'There's been quite a lot of talk of Schütter recently', and he later described how the commission for a piano concerto came about:

> One day, my wife and I visited Edmond de Stoutz and were looking for a work suitable for me to perform with his Zurich Chamber Orchestra. Meiny and his wife were regular visitors to our home, so it seemed natural to propose to de Stoutz that he give a first performance of a work by Schütter. He immediately agreed.[7]

Schütter wrote the work in 1985. The accompanying ensemble was restricted to strings alone. At 25 minutes in duration, it is by far his most substantial orchestral work. The premiere took place on 13 May 1986 in Theater 11 in Zurich, with Kramreiter and the Zurich Chamber Orchestra under the baton of Christof Escher.

The early 1980s were the time when the impact of long-lasting air pollution first became evident in the form of so-called 'forest dieback'. The emergence of 'green' parties, initially in Germany and then across the rest of Europe, was one consequence of this realisation, and an increasing concern for environmental protection initiated a shift of consciousness in society. Schütter's Piano Concerto took the destruction of the natural world as its inspiration. He recalled this time as follows:

> Back in the early 1980s, I intended writing a piano piece, a 'song without words' or, rather, a lament about how the spirits of forest and field were being driven away by the destruction of the environment. That became a precursor to my piano concerto. I had enjoyed an extremely happy childhood in my grandmother's chalet on the edge of the forest above Chur – it was an enchanting place. The chalet remains beautiful today, but I'm perturbed by the former meadows that have been built over and the cars that are there.
>
> In the 1950s, Hans Reinhart and Werner Kägi had commissioned me to make a performing version of Alfred Schlenker's opera *Die Flüchtlinge*, based on a Romantic tale by Hermann Hesse. I adopted some of the atmospheric elements of that work, I also drew on the forest environment that is so mythical to me, and from what for an older person like me is similarly mythical, namely my childhood. In this music, I overcome my fear of the hidden forces of Nature – of what is inexplicable and supernatural – and call back the spirits of the forests and the fields.[8]

Schütter also provided a more detailed explanation of the three movements of his concerto, which he refined in the year 2000:

---

[7] Tomás Kramreiter, 'Erinnerung an Meinrad Schütter', in Stoecklin, *Meinrad Schütter 1910–2006*, p. 174.
[8] Published in *ibid.*, pp. 126–27.

I. 'Cade il mondo' ('The world is falling') is a line from the libretto to Handel's opera *Agrippina*. I have placed it as a motto above the first movement, and it is encapsulated in a falling motif that is used repeatedly; it can also serve as a motto for the concerto as a whole. 'Cade il mondo' has something apocalyptic about it, and here refers to the dying forests of which people were becoming increasingly aware when I composed my concerto.

II. 'Les Adieux des bois' ('Farewell to the woods') The song by Brahms/ Groth at the close of the second movement of the concerto '… O, wüsst' ich doch den Weg zurück [, den lieben Weg zum Kinderland!' ('Oh, if only I knew the way back, to the dear land of childhood')'] is here a reminder of the rustling forests of my youth, which have since been decimated. This lifts everything into the realm of the transcendent, away from concrete environmental problems. Once you have grasped this immortal song with its ghostly bass, the labyrinthine twists and turns of its accompaniment and the wistfulness of its melody, you'll see the signpost of this longing for home.

III. The sequence 'Dies irae' in the last movement should be understood as an intensification of what has gone before it.[9]

Kramreiter later admitted that performing the work – which Schütter dedicated to him – was not unproblematical. It was Schütter's habit to revise his pieces constantly, even until just before a performance, and his scores were generally a patchwork of glued-on fragments of manuscripts paper, Tippex and overwritings (in some cases, his extant 'manuscripts' comprise photocopies of previous manuscripts that in turn bear all manner of corrections with ink and Tippex). Alexander Schaichet had already complained about the state of Schütter's scores over four decades earlier, and little had changed. Kramreiter suspects that the shoddy state of the material was one of the reasons why Edmond de Stoutz, who accepted Schütter's Piano Concerto for performance, had withdrawn from conducting it: 'Perhaps [he] wanted to avoid the hours of puzzling and calculating that I experienced when learning the work, because the score was in optical terms pure chaos.'[10]

The critic of the *Neue Zürcher Zeitung* was not overly enthusiastic after attending the first performance:

> The basic mood is pessimistic, the structure disjointed. The work is at times rhythmically gripping, but it sounds rather colourless and stand-offish. The piano part is virtuosic, often aggressive, and is contrasted with a heavy string section that sounds not too far removed from the dogged opulence and the luxuriant lustre of the unbroken Romanticism of the Elgar piece

[9] Published in *ibid.*, p. 127.
[10] Kramreiter, 'Erinnerung an Meinrad Schütter', p. 174.

that was played at the beginning of the concert [Elgar's *Serenade for Strings*]. Here as there, the orchestra sounded rather listless, occasionally imprecise in the details and in its coordination. Tomas Kramreiter was a technically accomplished soloist in the concerto, though he demonstrated a somewhat low level of commitment [...]. [11]

The critical response was quite different when the Piano Concerto was given its next performance, a full fourteen years later, again with the Zurich Chamber Orchestra but this time with the young French-Swiss Antoine Rebstein as soloist under the baton of Howard Griffiths. They also recorded the work for release on CD at the same time. In its review of the recording, the *Neue Zürcher Zeitung* claimed that the composer was 'long forgotten', but praised the way in which 'despite all its constructivism, [the concerto] sounds really sensual', noting how Rebstein was able to do justice to the 'apocalyptic sounds' of the dying forests and also 'revealed the hidden beauties of the score'.[12] The response was similarly positive in the Anglo-Saxon world. In a review for *Tempo*, Peter Palmer wrote:

> Schütter's fondness of reference and allusion is seen at its subtlest in the Piano Concerto of 1985. The first movement is subtitled 'Cade il mondo'. This phrase from the libretto of Handel's *Agrippina* is reflected in a descending musical phrase which determines the course and the character of the movement [Ex. 2 gives its first two pages]. Schütter's underlying concern – about the felling of the world's forests – also finds expression in a quotation from the second of Brahms's *Heimweh* songs [...]. In the finale the musico-ecological message is reinforced by the appearance of the *Dies irae* motif.[13]

Schütter composed little for voice in the 1980s – only four songs and a few small works for chorus – for his experience with musicians such as René Oswald and Kramreiter seems to have convinced him rather to engage with instrumental music of different kinds (a glance at his work catalogue confirms that he composed little instrumental or orchestral music in the years leading up to his retirement from the Opera House). The Piano Concerto is framed on either side by smaller works for string orchestra: the *Metamorphosis for String Orchestra* in 1975, which he revised thirteen years later, before its first performance; a brief *Concentus* for string orchestra followed in 1981, and then, perhaps emboldened by hearing the string textures accompanying his Piano Concerto, he wrote

[11] 'Ch. B.', 'Zwei Uraufführungen. Konzert des Zürcher Kammerorchesters im Theater 11', *Neue Zürcher Zeitung*, Vol. 207, No. 110, 15 May 1986.
[12] 'tsr' (Thomas Schacher), 'Klingendes Waldsterben', *Neue Zürcher Zeitung*, Vol. 221, No. 243, 18 October 2000.
[13] Palmer, *loc. cit.*, p. 56.

Ex. 2

Schütter at his desk in Küsnacht in 1989

three *Pastorales* in 1988 (the first and second for strings alone, the second featuring solo clarinet), all of which are based on the twelfth-century processional hymn 'Adorazione dei pastori' (a melody that fascinated Schütter and that can be heard threading its way through various works of his later years). *Concentus* and the second and third *Pastorales* were given their first performances in Seattle in the USA by the Northwest Chamber Orchestra under Eric Shumsky in 1990.

Schütter continued his series of works for René Oswald with *Nachtstücke I & II* ('Night Pieces') for flute, clarinet and piano or harpsichord (1987) and a *Humoreske* for clarinet and piano (1989). Besides his only Cello Sonata (1985), the 1980s also saw Schütter's first foray into the genre of the string quartet – a reworking of the *Metamorphosis* for strings made in 1988, as he later recalled:

> As far as I'm aware, I was one of the first, besides Hindemith and Strauss, to introduce the concept of 'metamorphosis' into music.[14] My first attempt at this was the final movement of my Five Variants and Metamorphosis of 1939. I took up the idea again in 1975 and wrote a short 6-minute Metamorphosis for string orchestra, which was premiered by Thomas Gartmann in 1988. In connection with this, I modified the composition into a version for string quartet. The title 'Metamorphosis' simply alludes

---

[14] Schütter was evidently unaware of Respighi's orchestral *Metamorphoseon*, a theme and twelve variations composed in 1930 for the 50th anniversary of the Boston Symphony Orchestra.

to the constant change, to how 'everything flows', to appearance and disappearance, or simply to ending something completely differently from how you began it. The beginning of each movement is based on the motif of the hymn 'Macht hoch die Tür, die Tor macht weit'.[15] The movements are related to one another. The motif of the song is, as it were, a link to a state of change.

Schütter composed his only full-scale String Quartet proper two years later, in 1990. It is cast in four movements, all in different forms of a *moderato* tempo (though couched in varied terms, from *Andante* to *Mässig bewegt*) and in a free atonal style with serial elements (Alban Berg's two quartets were perhaps Schütter's closest models here). It was not given its first public performance until 10 February 2019 in Basel (by the Ensemble Aventure of Freiburg im Breisgau), though it was recorded and released on compact disc by the Casal Quartet in 2006. This fondness for all things 'moderato' is typical of Schütter's tendency to leave the finer shadings of tempo and interpretation to the active discretion of his performers, though this multifarious 'moderato' is here often paired with a dancelike impetus that provides a contrasting lightness. Sometimes, the result can tend to the fragmentary and to ruptures in Schütter's musical narrative as if he wanted to rescind something that he had just uttered, leaving the listener to decipher his meaning. One reviewer of the String Quartet on CD found it perplexing, noting how Schütter 'often confronts disparate elements without ever trying to reconcile them', and while his immediate impression was that 'the music fails to satisfy', he admitted that 'I would like to hear more of it'.[16] In his review of that recording for *Tempo*, however, Peter Palmer was of a different opinion, writing that 'They [the Casal Quartet] make excellent musical sense of a shortish free-tonal piece (1990/96) by the prolific Hindemith pupil Meinrad Schütter [...]. Eclectic though [he] undoubtedly was [...] he produced an oeuvre to be reckoned with'.[17]

Besides the Piano Concerto, the 1980s also saw Schütter return to composing for piano solo, after having written almost nothing for his own instrument since the 1950s. After his *Variations on a Rhythm* for Tomás Kramreiter in 1982, he composed a few miniatures for piano and closed the decade with a cycle of four more, the *Four Pieces* of 1989, commissioned by my husband, Werner Stoecklin: I. 'On an old painting'; II. 'Study'; III. 'Dance of the Ghosts in the Scalära Valley'; and IV. '... or how time passes'. They were initially intended as pedagogical literature to

---

[15] Known in English as the hymn 'Fling wide the door' or 'Fling wide the gate".
[16] Hubert Culot, review of *Twentieth Century Swiss String Quartets* on MusicWeb International, www.musicweb-international.com (accessed 26 November 2023).
[17] Peter Palmer, review of three CDs of Swiss music, *Tempo*, No. 238 (October 2006), pp. 48–49, here p. 49.

Venera Zinsli: Meinrad Schütter in 1990

help encourage piano pupils to engage with modern music, though they proved too difficult except for the more gifted students. The first brings the 'Adorazione' motif that Schütter had used in his *Pastorales* for orchestra of the year before, the fourth is based on a twelve-note row, and the third is a virtuosic depiction of the legends mentioned earlier surrounding a particular valley just outside Chur.

Schütter celebrated his 80th birthday in 1990 in style, with a meal for friends and guests in the Seehof in Küsnacht, organised by Claudia, combined with a musical programme. The composer was in rude health and seems to have regarded the day as less of a closing gesture at the end of a career than as a signal to embark on new things. And that was indeed how things turned out.

12
Vagabond Poet: The Later Years

The contrasting responses to Schütter and his music – the 'pure chaos' of
the other-worldly dreamer that drove Kramreiter and others to despair,
and the constructivism and subtlety that were discernible to the reviewers
of the *Neue Zürcher Zeitung* and *Tempo* – are in fact reflective of the
determining aspects of Schütter's personality as a composer. For those
who knew him, it seems impossible to separate Schütter the man from his
work. Alexander Schaichet – the first musician of note to grapple with the
idiosyncrasies of Schütter's scores – had written to him in 1938 that 'I envy
you your ability to dream and your philosophical lingering'.[1] Composing
for Schütter was often indeed a kind of vagabond activity intricately linked
to his ability to distance himself from his quotidian circumstances and
let his thoughts wander. This quasi-meditative state was also responsible
for his frequent sense of disorientation in everyday life. Punctuality was
not his strong point, he was wont to get in the right train but in the wrong
direction, and on occasion was even able to get lost in his adopted city
of Zurich, unsure of whether he was on the east or the west bank of the
River Limmat. The manner of his attire was not dissimilar, betraying a
nonchalance that bordered on carelessness. There was, admittedly, also
an element of calculated theatricality to him; he was extremely quick-
witted, adept at verbal repartee and took delight in all manner of humour.
Schütter was also perfectly capable of directing his wit against others,
though rarely with any intention to hurt, and his own sensitivity to ill-will
led to him erecting a certain ironic distance to others. This irony was often
paired with a sense of melancholy that lies like a veil over much of his
work. 'For me', he once said, 'the world with its intrigues and shortcomings
was never of importance, though in the long run, this leads to solitariness.
As it says in the Bible, that world is one in which the Devil has his say.'

Schütter liked to think of himself most as a 'poet', a composer of
distilled lyrical moments, and he generally preferred the small-scale to
the monumental. So it was not surprising that he loved aphorisms, nor
that he wrote many works that are extremely concise and pithy (and in
their brevity are accordingly problematic to interpret). His personality

---

[1] Letter from Schaichet to Schütter, 15 June 1938.

Schütter in 1998

also made him naturally averse to adhering to any sets of rules ('I never threw myself into the arms of any particular system', he remarked in 2004). He was a 'homo ludens' – a man full of curiosity who would take what appealed to him from whatever systems or styles were at hand. Schütter had begun in late-Romanticism and Expressionism, moving into Neo-Classicism, and later used note-rows, polyrhythmic structures, the Fibonacci series, quotations and collage whenever they suited him. Such formal elements, however, like his use of tonal centres within a largely free-atonal context, provide thematic markers and a means of orientation for the listener (and can also reveal themselves as the constructivism and subtlety noted by the critics).

Postmodernism arrived on the Swiss music scene towards the end of the 1980s, somewhat later than in the Anglo-American world. The avantgarde that had dominated central European music gave way to stylistic pluralism and a heterogeneity of expression. Schütter now found himself in familiar territory once more, for postmodernism favoured expressivity and emotion, no longer considering them regressive as had so often been the case in the years before.

These musical upheavals in the closing years of the twentieth century seemed to release new creative energies in Schütter. In the years between his Piano Concerto and the turn of the century he composed some twenty chamber-music works, seventeen choral compositions (both *a cappella* and with instrumental accompaniment), eighteen songs with piano and six songs with instrumental accompaniment. It was the first time since his intense engagement with the Lied in the 1930s that Schütter had composed so much for voice and piano. The turn of the millennium also saw him return to his Symphony, which he had begun in the late 1930s and had revised and extended already twice before, in 1965 and 1970.

Schütter's chamber music of the 1990s included his first-ever works for horn – a *Bagatelle* for Horn and Piano of 1993/95 and a Romance for the same instruments from 1993/2001, both short pieces only two minutes long. But Schütter's most significant chamber work of the new decade was a result of his continued fascination with the clarinet – in this case, three of them. He composed his Trio for Three Clarinets (or basset horns) in 1992 to a commission from his old friend Philipp Zinsli of Chur. It was inspired by a picture carved onto a capital of the portal of Vézelay Cathedral that Schütter saw while on a trip he made to Burgundy, together with Zinsli and his wife, Verena: it depicts a pilgrim, stooped down, tying his shoelaces with his foot on a pedestal. The Trio is in four movements (1. *Allegro moderato*; 2. Intermezzo, 'In the Garden'; 3. Litany, 'The Pilgrim's Poor Footwear'; 4. Canon, *Poco allegro*). Schütter later described the work as follows:

> It's the shoelace motif that we find in the most diverse artistic depictions along the old pilgrims' route to Santiago de Compostela, which also went through Vézelay [...]. This became the kernel of my Litany, around which the other movements are arranged in suite form. The short first movement is followed by an intermezzo, 'In the Garden', in which I incorporated quotations from Olivier Messiaen's *Catalogue d'Oiseaux*. The third movement, 'Litany', takes as its topic the shoestring image described above. There are several short pauses in the music, and sections depicting sacred earnestness alternate with a mechanical winding motion. The finale is a brief canon.[2]

The Trio was given a brilliant first performance in 1993 by the Calamus Trio at a house concert of the Zinslis' in Chur. They played it several times thereafter on a series of concerts throughout the canton of Graubünden

[2] CD booklet text in Meinrad Schütter, *Kammermusik und instrumental begleitete Gesänge 1939–98*, Swisspan 510 316, Zurich, 2000.

and elsewhere. It was recorded for compact disc in the year 2000, though by a different trio, this one comprising Hans Rudolf Stalder, Mathias Müller and Elmar Schmid.[3]

Just as Karin Ott, Tomás Kramreiter and René Oswald had inspired Schütter in the 1980s, his creative intensity in the 1990s was a result of his acquaintance with a new generation of performers who had discovered his music, among them the mezzo-soprano Stefania Huonder, the baritone Michael Leibundgut, the flautist Carsten Hustedt, the Polish clarinettist Romuald Gołębiowski and the Fennica Trio (Helena Maffli-Nissinen, piano; Dorota Sosnowska, violin; Jarmo Vainio, cello). The Trio was active internationally and regularly featured Polish and Finnish works on its programmes. Schütter wrote his Piano Trio for them in 1996. He explained at the time: 'I worked using a note row after the manner of Dallapiccola, which allowed me to alter it freely and according to the sensual qualities of the sound I wanted – it's conceived as a kind of "italianità" that is dear to me.'[4] The Trio is cast in a single movement with rapidly shifting tempi. Lyrical interjections seem to evoke examples of the genre from earlier epochs. The premiere took place on 4 October 1998 in Villeneuve, in a programme that also featured works by Aarre Merikanto, Edvard Grieg and Paul Juon and was subsequently broadcast on Swiss French Radio. Schütter was especially drawn to the warm tone of his friend Jarmo Vainio, and they often played chamber music together for as long as Schütter still played the piano. Otherwise they both smoked incessantly (Vainio preferring cigarillos, Schütter cigarettes), and were both fond of a glass of wine while discussing God and the world – a practice they kept up until shortly before Schütter's death.

Schütter's music was still little known at this time, for the simple reason that it was unpublished and largely unrecorded and thus inaccessible to anyone who didn't know how to contact the composer directly. Three events changed that in the course of the 1990s. When perusing Schütter's songs – of which there were over two dozen from the previous half century – I was surprised by their quality, and decided – not least on the express recommendation of my husband, Werner, shortly before his death in January 1992 – that I should take active steps to ensure that they were rescued from their oblivion. Together with Francis Schneider, the head of a relatively new Swiss music publishing company by the name of Nepomuk, we decided to publish a series of songbooks. The first two volumes of six songs each were published in late 1991. Nepomuk went on to publish numerous other works by Schütter, for piano and various chamber-music

---

[3] *Ibid.*
[4] *Ibid.*

ensembles. Nepomuk was later taken over by Breitkopf & Härtel, which has kept the music of Schütter in its catalogue to this day.

The song volumes published by Nepomuk were soon acquired by the Zurich Central Library, which has the designated task of collecting the work of all composers resident in Canton Zurich (thus including Schütter). This acquisition led to a series of conversations that culminated in Schütter donating his music manuscripts to the library in 1995. The collection was catalogued, and the catalogue placed online, thereby aiding the accessibility of Schütter's music to musicians and scholars both present and future.[5] The third event was the successive release of compact discs of Schütter's music, beginning with a selection of his songs on the Uranus label in 1997[6] (a 'quietly sparkling collection', wrote Peter Palmer in *Tempo*[7]).

This renewed interest in his songs prompted Schütter to return to the genre, composing another dozen songs in the course of the decade, including his only two song-cycles. In 1990 he was commissioned to set several texts by the contemporary Graubünden poet Flandrina von Salis. He chose five from her volume of poems published in 1974 under the title *Phoenix – Wegstrecken der Liebe* ('Phoenix – Paths of Love'), which also gave him the title for his cycle: *Phoenix* for mezzo-soprano and piano (1991); Ex. 3 gives its opening. It was first performed by Stefania Huonder, accompanied by Beatrice Kurth, in Malans, some ten miles north of Chur, on 26 October 1991.

Schütter's second cycle was *Chanzuns de la not* ('Songs of the Night'; 1994), which comprise settings of three poems in Rumansh by the Engadine poet Andri Peer. Rumansh was Stefania Huonder's mother tongue, which gave her performances of Schütter's Rumansh settings a unique flavour – in the song recitals that she and I gave together at the time, Schütter's early Rumansh song *Dumonda*[8] became almost what one might term a 'hit'. So when we were engaged to record a programme of songs for Radio Rumansh, Schütter decided to compose three more for us. As his texts, he chose three by Andri Peer and brought them together to form a cycle. Stefania Huonder and I recorded the *Chanzuns de la not* in May 1994 and first performed them in Chur on 20 September 1995 in a concert celebrating Schütter's 85th birthday. The second and third of these two songs were also included on the CD *Hesperus* in 2002 (with Michael Leibundgut, bass, accompanied by me) and featuring songs by Schütter,

---

[5] The shelfmark of the collection is Mus NL 2; the catalogue (which is downloadable) can be found by searching for 'Meinrad Schütter' at https://zbcollections.ch/home (accessed October 2023).
[6] Meinrad Schütter, *Lieder*, Uranus URA 602, Zurich, 1997, with Karin Ott, Stefanie Huonder and Otto Georg Linsi accompanied variously by Janka Wyttenbach and Ute Stoecklin.
[7] Peter Palmer, *loc. cit.* (2001), p. 56.
[8] Discussed on pp. 45–48, above.

Ex. 3

Schoeck and Scartazzini. Schütter's songs were praised for his sensitivity to the texts, and the recording was named 'Disc of the Month' in January 2003 by the website MusicWeb International.[9]

Schütter's account of the *Chanzuns de la not* includes an unusually personal note at the close:

> My choice of text was influenced on the one hand by my friendship with Andri Peer, which began many years ago,[10] and on the other hand by the colourful, sensual pathos of his poems, which influenced the evolving manner in which I treated my musical material. The vocal line is at times sung, at others half-sung or even spoken. The piano part is of equal importance, sometimes constricted in its elucidation of the melodic line, while at other times quite independent.
>
> 'L'Alba' ('Dawn') is an introverted love lyric;
>
> 'Zona dal plaschair' ('Zone of Pleasure'): here I have tried to shift the emotional exuberance of the text onto another plane by alternating sung, half-sung and spoken passages;

---

[9] At www.musicweb-international.com/classrev/2003/Jan03/Hesperos.htm (accessed October 2023).
[10] The circumstances are outlined on p. 61, above.

Flandrina von Salis and Schütter at a song recital chez *Zinsli, 1993*

'Favuogn' ('Windy Morning') is a predominantly quiet song, full of inner tension. The 'Dies irae' appears as a brief, monodic quotation in the piano part.

A composer who has grown up in an old episcopal city will cope better with the toil, headaches and disjunction of our times through his awareness of the transience of his existence. He will see the tribulations of life with a greater sense of distance.

The mid-1990s were indeed a time when the 'transience of existence' weighed heavily on Schütter, as they were marked by the death of several people to whom he was very close. His longstanding friend and patron Philipp Zinsli died in mid-1995. He had been a vital conversation partner to Schütter over the years, unafraid to confront him in their many discussions, whether about music or politics; his loss seemed to throw Schütter unexpectedly off-balance. In the space of only a few days he composed a seven-minute piece for clarinet and organ to be performed at Zinsli's funeral on 9 June, *Consolazione*. It was played by Martin Imfeld, accompanied at the organ by the composer.

An even more fundamental change to Schütter's life was brought about by the increasingly poor health of his wife, the full facts of which remained unclear to him until it was already too late. When the imminence of her death became obvious in her final weeks, he was helpless. Claudia died of cancer on 18 February 1996. She had long been by far the most important person in his life. His friends now stood by him, helping him to organise his new daily life in what was an ever-expanding chaos. He began to cook for himself, though his insistence on smoking in a kitchen with a gas cooker was a source of no little unease among the other residents of his small apartment block. Nor was Schütter's habit of tucking unpaid utilities bills, correspondence and concert programmes behind the tiled heating stove in the living room conducive to running an orderly household. His friends consequently began looking for a retirement home to which he might move in the near future. They found one in the Wangensbach Retirement Home in Küsnacht, which is located in a park above Lake Zurich with a beautiful panoramic view, but only a few minutes by foot from the heart of the village and the local amenities. It stands next to an old country house that had briefly been the home of the nineteenth-century Swiss poet Conrad Ferdinand Meyer – a fact that in itself made the place appealing to Schütter. He moved there in 1999, in his ninetieth year, though in fact he was still 'out and about' most of the time, hardly ever in his new home, but travelling or living with friends in Basel instead, and composing.

13
Chamber Music in Vilnius

In 1996, the tenor Otto Georg Linsi commissioned Schütter to write a work for contralto, tenor, flute and piano for performance at a Swiss Cultural Week to be held in Kyiv in Ukraine. The result was the chamber cantata *Der Steinsammler* ('The Stone-Collector'), to poems by Nelly Sachs, and was first performed on 22 April 1997. Schütter followed this work immediately with another Sachs setting, the song *Schmetterling* ('Butterfly') for mezzo-soprano and piano. Schütter was at this time increasingly interested in the ideas of Hans Kayser (1891–1964), a German music-theorist and sometime student of Arnold Schoenberg who had posited 'harmonic vibration' as an ordering principle and had endeavoured to find common formal ideas in music, architecture, cosmology and much more – though Schütter's embrace of certain harmonic ideas derived from Kayser in his Nelly Sachs settings was tempered by his preference for dodecaphonic procedures. The first performance of *Schmetterling* was given by Stefania Huonder, accompanied by me, in Ratzeburg in Schleswig Holstein in 1997. Schütter travelled there with us, and used the opportunity to get better acquainted with northern Germany, its forests and lakes, its towns with their Hanseatic traditions and redbrick Gothic buildings, and its music. Our programme comprised songs by Schoeck, Schütter, Sibelius and Grieg – four composers whose work was spread over one-and-a-half centuries, but all of whom were deeply influenced by the landscapes of their respective native regions; the two Swiss composers were unsurprisingly new to the local critics.

The flautist at the first performance of *Der Steinsammler* had been Carsten Hustedt, who had begun working with fellow musicians in the former eastern bloc not long after the fall of the Berlin Wall in 1989. He performed there regularly, and now became a keen advocate of Schütter's music. Schütter accordingly wrote several compositions for him in the ensuing years, and was featured increasingly on Hustedt's programmes in the former Soviet bloc. Hustedt taught each year at courses and seminars in Vilnius, the capital city of Lithuania, and asked Schütter to compose a piece for flute and cello for his courses there in 1998. Schütter accordingly

*Ute Stoecklin, Schütter and Stefania Huonder at a song recital
in Ratzeburg in Germany, 27 September 1997*

composed his Duo for Flute and Cello after a scene from Aristophanes'
The Frogs, which he explained as follows:

> It's a piece of tone painting that resulted from the two instruments featured
> in the commission, flute and cello, and the fact that I happened to be
> reading the comedies of Aristophanes at the time, in particular his *Frogs*.
> The first, burlesque scenes of the journey undertaken to the Underworld
> by Dionysus and his servant Xanthias provided me with the original
> scenario on which I based my composition, though I then moved away
> from it, focussing only on the shape of the overall piece. – You could
> perhaps describe it as an ironic scherzo.

This highly fragmentary work reveals Schütter the aphorist. Calm, lyrical
passages are contrasted with skittish, dance-like sections, and the work
closes in the same tempo and dialogic manner as it had opened. The
Duo was first performed in Vilnius on 26 November 1998 in the Palais
Mickiewicz, a sixteenth-century house in the old city. It was eight years
since Lithuania had regained its independence, with reconstruction and
renovation still in their early stages. There were ice floes on the River Neris
that November, Vilnius was covered in snow, the temperature was minus
15 degrees Celsius, and the concert hall was unheated. The musicians
rehearsed in their winter coats. But on the evening of the concert itself, the
hall was filled to capacity and the audience enthusiastic. Besides Schütter,
the programme featured works by the Neapolitan Giuseppe Giordani
(1751–98), the Lithuanian Onutė Narbutaitė[1] and the Swiss Thomas
Demenga.[2] Schütter was very pleased with the performance, though he
felt his own piece was a little too long and declared his intention to shorten
it. He was now 88 years old but in rude health and feeling adventurous.
He had travelled little outside Italy and the German-speaking countries
and was fascinated both by the city of Vilnius in its current transitional
state and by the musicians he met, first and foremost the musicologist
Ona Narbutienė,[3] her daughter, the abovementioned composer Onutė
Narbutaitė, and the violist Audronė Pšibilskienė.[4] But everywhere he went
about the city he found people to talk to – on the street, in museums, in
bookshops and restaurants, conversing in either his clumsy English or his

---

[1] Onutė Narbutaitė (born 1956), Lithuanian composer, studied in Vilnius and came to prominence in
the west after the fall of the Iron Curtain; her fellow Lithuanian, the conductor Mirga Gražinytė-Tyla,
has championed her work in Birmingham and elsewhere.
[2] Thomas Demenga (born 1954), Swiss cellist and composer, born in Bern, studied in New York with
Mstislav Rostropovich and others.
[3] Ona Narbutienė (1930–2007), Lithuanian musicologist; she was deported in her teens to Siberia,
returned after Stalin's death and studied at the Vilnius Conservatoire. Her daughter is the composer
Onutė Narbutaitė.
[4] Audronė Pšibilskienė, Lithuanian violist, born 1946.

better French. He was rarely tired, though he did feel the cold when he visited the unheated museums of the city. And he enjoyed the local vodka.

Schütter loved to write pieces for special dates, whether Christmas or the birthdays of friends (assuming, of course, that he didn't simply forget about the upcoming occasion, which he often did). One such work for Christmas was *Aus den Weihnachtsbriefen an Frieda Mermet* of 1996 ('From the Christmas Letters to Frieda Mermet') for speaker, flute, string quartet and piano to texts by the early twentieth-century Swiss writer Robert Walser.[5] It was only Schütter's second Walser setting – though as it happens, its predecessor, his song *Reisen* ('Travelling' or 'Voyages') of 1991, had also featured a spoken, central section. Schütter chose fragments from the letters that Robert Walser wrote to his close friend Frieda Mermet, who worked as a washerwoman in the psychiatric institute Bellelay in the Jura.

Roman Brotbeck has written as follows about Schütter's 'Christmas Letters':

> This music consists of five short pieces that relate closely to the spoken passages and are exemplary for the heterogeneity of Meinrad Schütter's compositional style: chorale-like passages and periods are set alongside a piano style reminiscent of Max Reger with its Baroque-like figurations, while at the same time revealing a distorted counterpoint whose harmony often utilises triads and tetrads but whose tonal sense is veiled by the use of dissonant tones. [...] Schütter's music comes across as if an improvising musician is spinning out the thought-processes of the texts [...].[6]

In 1998, Schütter made a second version of this work for speaker, flute and piano, in which form it was first performed by Carsten Hustedt and me in 1999. A year later, Hustedt commissioned Schütter to write three cadenzas each for the flute concertos Op. 29 by Carl Stamitz and K313 by Mozart. Schütter explained how the commission had come about:

> When these cadenzas were requested of me [...] I was asked: 'What does Mozart mean to you, what does Stamitz mean to you?' [...]. No original cadenzas exist for these two works, and I endeavoured to translate them into our contemporary musical language, to interpret them and reflect on them and to use the means of extended tonality and recent playing techniques, some of which were impossible in their time, to evoke a fictive hike on which one might imagine conducting a conversation with these two composers in a spirit of wit and humour.

---

[5] Robert Walser (1878–1956), Swiss writer, spent his last 27 years in psychiatric institutions. He is regarded today as one of the leading Modernists in the German-speaking world.
[6] Roman Brotbeck, *Töne und Schälle. Robert Walser-Vertonungen 1912 bis 2021*, Brill Fink, Paderborn, 2021, pp. 506–7.

These cadenzas were given their first performances by Hustedt in Stuttgart in January 2001, accompanied by the St Christopher Chamber Orchestra of Vilnius under Donatus Katkus. At Hustedt's suggestion, Schütter later brought the six cadenzas together as pieces for solo flute under the title *Promenades à Mannheim*.

Schütter loved hiking in the mountains – in his home canton of Graubünden, in the Italian-speaking Ticino, and also in the Upper Valais, specifically in the Goms Valley near the border with Italy, where he spent many summers. In 1999, while staying at the historic Post Hotel in Münster in Goms, he composed his *Gommer Suite*, a trio for flute, violin and viola comprising ten miniatures that he once jokingly called his 'Little Alpine Symphony'. The Suite was commissioned by the violist Hans Georg Büchel and his trio Diletto Musicale from Bonn, and they first performed it in the small Baroque church in the picturesque village of Niederwald in the Goms Valley on 20 July 1999 at the twentieth gathering of the annual 'Goms Evening Concerts'. The suite describes a hike through the Goms – the wide, high-lying valley of the young Rhône with its picturesque Valais villages nestled in alpine slopes, their wooden houses burnt black by the sun.

These ten miniatures are couched in a dry but colourful, transparent style that seems to trace out the alpine landscape. There are relaxed canons in which there are brief flickers of motifs from church music such as 'Ein' feste Burg' or 'Adeste fideles', and the Suite ends with a characteristically humorous waltz that was inspired by the old tomcat of the owners of the Post Hotel in Goms, Ruth and Simon Aellig. 'The canons here are only the remnant of an idea', claimed Schütter; 'their references are first and foremost through-composed'.

14

A New Century and a Symphony

Schütter was now settled in his retirement home in Küsnacht, but he continued to carry out his duties as organist at the Dreifaltigkeitskirche in Zollikon just outside Zurich, lugging overflowing folders of music back and forth by bus, train or on foot, regardless of the state of the weather, in the summer heat or the winter snows. He always took a lot of music with him; if he felt on the day that he didn't want to improvise, then he had enough material with him to play before the service.

He had a small flat in his retirement home and had settled in quickly. As was his wont, he charmed everyone around him, whether fellow retirees or staff, received many visits from old friends, and sometimes made new friends too. He took a contemplative, occasionally ironic view of his current place of abode. In July 2004 he remarked:

> I consider a retirement home to be a highly interesting field for experimentation, because it is a railway siding that's both cheerful and uneasy, with two options: death or life. People see through this and try and ignore it by making banal observations about their material circumstances. That's why they get bored!'

In 1999, the year he moved into his retirement home, Schütter returned to the one-movement symphony he had worked on intermittently over more than 60 years, bringing together all his sketches and drafts into a work for a first performance in time for his 90th birthday the following year. After making initial sketches in 1937, Schütter had finished a provisional version in Rome in 1939. He recalled: 'I remember the days I spent in Anzio by the sea in January 1939 when it felt as though a ship was sailing past, shrouded constantly by banks of fog in a scene whose ghostly, unreal atmosphere was like that of Wagner's *Flying Dutchman*'. The political situation in Europe was already precarious, and the mood of his symphony, thus Schütter, was determined by an 'accumulation of things still to come'. Over the ensuing decades, however, the music of this symphony underwent several major changes.

In 1947, the Swiss composer and conductor Hans Haug had been scheduled to conduct the premiere of Schütter's symphony at the Zurich Radio Studio, but the performance was cancelled 'for technical reasons'

Schütter at the organ in Zollikon in May 2002

not long before it was due to take place. This disruption sealed the fate of the work for the next half-century. Schütter put it aside, revised it in the 1960s, and then made sketches for a new version in 1970 (including new sections using dodecaphony). But he found the results unsatisfactory and so did not pursue the matter further for the moment. The version that he completed in 1999 was in large part quite new and, in the spirit of relaxed disillusionment that came with his advancing age, Schütter declared that the work had undergone 'a strange transformation'.

The Symphony was already short in its early versions, and in the course of its gestation it became even shorter and increasingly concise. As he distanced himself ever further from the subject-matter of its origins, he found himself in a position to exert ever more severe self-criticism. In formal terms, the Symphony perhaps has most in common with a Baroque single-movement *sinfonia*. The Neo-Classical 'concessions' in the original work (or 'complaisances', as Schütter called them), which were perfectly valid in the stylistic context of the 1930s and 1940s, were now largely discarded, only constituting a spectral presence in the final version. Later, Schütter derived twelve-note rows from his earlier themes and thereafter even reduced them to a single seven-note motif with fixed harmonies; it provides him with the material for two themes that run throughout the work in fragmentary form. One of them serves to prepare the music for its conclusion, which remains essentially as Schütter had already composed it back in 1939.

In retrospect, the music of the Symphony is a kind of folder containing a collection of small, notated events and memories that flicker into consciousness, not unlike diary excerpts that are directly related to Schütter's personal life. It is a music of ruptures, stylistic mixtures and shifts in perspective, all of which resulted from its long period of gestation, and which came to constitute – so Schütter himself admitted – a kind of autobiography with all its inherent contradictions ('it's my life', he said). But it by no means constitutes some random juxtaposition of musical fragments, for they cohere in small, self-enclosed formal sections that are contrasted with one another.

Schütter discussed all these matters on alpine hikes that we undertook together in the summer of 1999, a year before the Symphony was given its first performance. On one such occasion, we stopped for refreshments in the high-lying restaurant Turrahus in the Safiertal in Canton Graubünden – a region he knew well – and the landscapes prompted him to talk about many things past, including about the symphony that was drawing to a close. He freely admitted his reticence in providing indications to his performers as to how they should play his music, preferring to let them find their way by themselves. The Symphony is a prime example of this *laissez-faire* approach.

He attended several of the rehearsals of the work in Chur in 2000, but the premiere, given on 22 September by the Orchesterverein Chur under the baton of Luzius Müller, prompted mostly incomprehension. Three years later, however, Michael Eidenbenz writing in the main Swiss musicological journal *dissonanz* offered a more considered opinion of the work:

> 'The opening material regrettably doesn't appear again later', says the composer today when looking through his score, as if what he had created had somehow eluded his control and taken on a life of its own during the creative process [...]. Schütter's superficially detached composure is far removed from the loquacious commentaries offered by many another contemporary composer today – and naturally stands in stark contrast to the rigid control exerted on the course of the work, and the 'coherence' of its energies that Schütter tirelessly scrutinises. The work does not follow any conventional formal model, instead bringing together different musical elements into a structure that is characterised by contrasts, interruptions and the resumption of things familiar [...]. These particles, fragments, the often rapidly shifting tempi, the dynamic drive in the large orchestra that is repeatedly brought to a pause by marvellous solos for clarinet and violin – all of this is organised within a delicately structured, yet coherent arc that ultimately makes this 20-minute composition an incredibly rich, vivid picture.[1]

The city of Chur commemorated Schütter's 90th birthday with several events, including a performance of his *Grosse Messe* in which Theophil Handschin conducted the Chur Chamber Choir, and a chamber concert at which four composers from the canton presented one first performance each: Robert Grossmann, Martin Derungs, Oreste Zanetti and Urban Derungs – a programme that delighted Schütter.

The municipality of Küsnacht – Schütter's current home – also organised a birthday concert in the Seehof (the local cultural centre that also serves as the home of the C. G. Jung Institute), featuring the Fennica Trio with Romuald Gołębiowski (clarinet), the mezzo Stefania Huonder, the baritone Michael Leibundgut and myself as piano accompanist. The programme included the first performances of several piano pieces by Schütter and the Swiss premiere of his *Separate Einbildungen* ('Separate Fictions') from 1999 for clarinet, violin, cello and piano, based on texts by the Polish poet Stanisław Jerzy Lec (1909–66). The hall was full, and many of Schütter's surviving friends were in attendance.

Towards the end of 2001, Schütter became ill. A lifetime of intensive smoking was finally taking its toll, resulting in peripheral artery disease –

[1] Michael Eidenbenz, 'Freiheit und Glück einer eigenen Sprache. Der Komponist Meinrad Schütter', *dissonanz*, No. 81 (June 2003), pp. 20–26.

*The birthday concert in Küsnacht in 2000. From left: Jarmo Vainio,
Helena Maffli-Nissinen, Stefania Huonder, Ute Stoecklin, Schütter,
Dorota Sosnowska, Romuald Gołębiowski and Michael Leibundgut*

also known as 'smoker's leg', in which the flow of blood to the limbs is
drastically reduced. The doctors had to operate. It all proceeded smoothly,
but complications followed, including a viral infection. He had a high
fever and fell into a delirium in which fear, horror and meek surrender
alternated. It seemed that he could not possibly live much longer, and
there followed a week of goodbyes. On what seemed inevitably to be his
final day, he attained the clarity to say that he had done everything he'd
wanted, that it was time to go, and so he bade his last farewells. But that
same afternoon he got a nurse to ring me, he asked her to hand him the
receiver, and then told me quite calmly: 'I've decided to go on living'. It
was astonishing, but somehow characteristic of Schütter's sense of the
theatrical.

His recovery was slow but steady, and by 1 September 2002 he was
well enough to attend a portrait concert dedicated to him in Rünenberg
in Canton Baselland and to participate in the discussion that was held
afterwards. Schütter was now clearly enjoying his 'second start' in life,
though he was more withdrawn than before, and lived for weeks at a
time in Basel, away from his actual home in Küsnacht. Two days after
the concert in Rünenberg, a Meinrad Schütter Society was founded in
Binningen in Canton Baselland in order to promote his music and support
publications and recordings. Later that same year, I set up the 'Concert
Gallery Maison 44' in an *art nouveau* house at Steinenring 44 in the

After a Liederabend in Basel: Schütter, Ute Stoecklin,
the composer Andrea Scartazzini and the baritone Michael Leibundgut

centre of Basel. The idea behind it was inter-disciplinary, the aim being to combine contemporary art, music, literature and scholarship in a single venue. The gallery hosted nine to twelve concerts each season, with song-recitals having a core function in the programme. Schütter often attended, and his own works were performed there on a regular basis. Over time, he essentially became the composer-in-residence of the gallery.

In 2003, Michael Eidenbenz's long article on Schütter in the journal *dissonanz*[2] included as an appendix the catalogue of Schütter's works that I had begun working on a full ten years earlier – a Sisyphean task, given Schütter's decades-old, haphazard manner of documenting his *œuvre*, though it finally enabled us to determine just how much he had actually composed. Published by the Swiss Musicians' Association, *dissonanz* was distributed to all its members, many of whom had known Schütter for many years but had no idea just how productive a composer he had been. His old colleague Robert Suter, the sometime chair of the Basel branch of the ISCM, had known Schütter back at the Zurich Opera House but now wrote to him to express his astonishment at having been oblivious of the extent of his output.

It was in Basel in these years that Schütter got to know the sculptor Ludwig Stocker (born in 1932). They visited each other often, with Schütter also spending time in Stocker's studio, where the latter began to work

---

[2] *Ibid.*

Ludwig Stocker, Ute Stoecklin and Schütter in Stocker's studio in Basel, 2003.
In the background on the left is Stocker's bust of Schütter

on a bust of the composer. The Art Association of Binningen organised
an exhibition of Stocker's works in 2004 entitled 'Culture reflects upon
itself' that brought together sculpture and music and incorporated the
Swiss first performances of Schütter's organ pieces *De Leonardo Pisano*
and *Meditation*, played by Pia Blum.

Schütter was soon immersed in a large-scale commission from the
Schlaraffia in Zurich, which resulted in his fifteen-minute *Fanfares* for
three trumpets, two horns, tenor trombone and timpani, which was first
performed on 23 October 2004 at the Schlaraffia quinquennial congress
held that year at the Congress House in Lucerne. Schütter was busy
with smaller-scale works, too: *Am Gürtel Orions* ('On Orion's Belt') and
Grundungen ('Foundations'), both for cello and speaker, are settings of texts
by the Swiss writer Andreas Neeser, who was the head of the Literaturhaus
in Aarau at the time and with whom Schütter had recently become
acquainted. Schütter then embarked on a quartet for oboe, trumpet,
bassoon and cello, commissioned by a friend, the art historian Fritz
Hermann, who lived not far from Schütter's retirement home in Küsnacht,
and who had specifically requested that unusual instrumentation. The
commission had been intended for performance on Hermann's birthday,
2 February 2005, which is also the feast of Candlemas in the Catholic
Church; Hermann had accordingly requested the work to convey a sense
of moving 'from darkness to the light'. However, he had given Schütter

only two months for the composition, which was insufficient; he did not complete the work until the following May. The Quartet is cast in a single movement and uses several note-rows, although not in any strict fashion; it ends with 'fanfares of light', in line with the original commission. In the end, its first performance was given not on Hermann's birthday, but on Schütter's own, at a concert held in Küsnacht on 1 October 2005 to celebrate his 95th. It was performed alongside Schütter's early *Serenade* for voice and string trio of 1934, songs and piano pieces, several of the latter also in their first public airing.

Schütter's most important premiere of this year, however, was not of one of his latest works, but of *Medea*. I had tried for many years to encourage him to make an abridged version of this, his only opera, extracting either a suite from it or some other excerpt that might be performed in a chamber setting. He toyed with the idea several times, but always abandoned it – until the winter of 2004–5, at a time when he was already often very unwell, and he finally gave me permission to make an abridged version for piano and four soloists, cutting its original two hours down to 55 minutes. The chorus has an essential role in the opera, so its absence required a narrator to mediate the action. The actor Peter Niklaus Steiner from Zurich was engaged to sketch out the text for the narrator and to speak it in performance. He visited Schütter in his old-age home in Küsnacht and suggested incorporating passages from Robinson Jeffers' adaptation of *Medea*. Schütter agreed, and this abridged *Medea* was finally performed in the Museum der Kulturen in Basel on 1 and 2 November 2005. The performers were Kimberley Brockman (soprano), Roswitha Müller (mezzo), Hans-Jürg Rickenbacher (tenor), Michael Leibundgut (bass), Hans Adolfsen (piano) and Peter Niklaus Steiner (narrator), with the rehearsals under the direction of Adolfsen. Even in this abridged version, the performances were able to offer a concise, closely focussed impression of the overall opera while conveying its broad dramatic arc. The two performances in Basel were a considerable success. They were also the last time that Schütter was able to appear in public at a concert of his own music.

In his review for *dissonanz*, Michael Eidenbenz wrote as follows:

> As in his songs, we find here an apparent contradiction between a seemingly rigid compositional technique and a suppleness of melody and harmony that is accommodating both to a meticulous expressiveness in the details and to grand impassioned gestures such as we find in the figure of Medea herself [...]. [The music] oscillates between emotional proximity and judicious distance, between subjective understanding and an objectifying perspective. This is characteristic of both [Schütter's]

Schütter in his last years

approach to the myth and, ultimately, also to how we too engage with the work of this maverick on the local composing scene – a composer who has now belatedly, but impressively, also revealed himself as a creator of music theatre.[3]

During his final weeks, Schütter often listened to the recording of the concert performance of his *Medea*, but always heard it in his head (he told me) in its full, orchestral version. He never mentioned the piano accompaniment, but only discussed the individual instruments whenever he referred to a particular passage or wanted to explain something.

[3] Michael Eidenbenz, 'Ehrenrettung für eine vergessene Oper', *dissonanz*, No. 93 (March 2006), pp. 31–32.

On one occasion, referring to a passage in the wind, he remarked with delight that 'No one else back then would have written it like that!' The only other work that occupied Schütter in these final weeks was Wagner's *Parsifal*. One evening, not long after the second Basel performance of *Medea*, surrounded by a small group of friends, Schütter went to the piano and started improvising slowly from *Parsifal* – a work that had fascinated him for decades, especially for its focus on pity – 'Mitlied' – and to which he used to refer as 'Wagner's *Faust*'. He then began playing through the vocal score of the work, quite lucidly, sometimes conducting along with one hand, singing the motifs and enthusiastically pointing out transitional passages. When he had finished, he closed the piano lid – something that he otherwise never did.

One final performance of *Medea* was given at the City Theatre in Schütter's home city of Chur on 20 December 2005, though its composer was no longer able to attend. Meinrad Schütter died just under a month later, in Küsnacht, on 12 January 2006. In his final weeks he had been troubled by nightmares about his mother. But when it came, the close of his life was marked by acceptance and affirmation. Shortly before the end, he simply said: 'It was magnificent, wasn't it?'.

Afterword
Meinrad Schütter: The Music and the Man

CHRIS WALTON

The composing profile of Meinrad Schütter was really a tale of two careers. The first followed the standard pattern of so many of his Swiss composing colleagues in the decades before his birth. Born in the alpine provinces, he underwent initial training in his native land before studying abroad (though in Schütter's case, financial hardship necessitated self-study), then returned home to earn his living as a pianist and conductor, with composition relegated to the sidelines. This was the pattern established already in the nineteenth century by Swiss composers such as Theodor Fröhlich (1803–36), Johann Carl Eschmann (1826–82) and Volkmar Andreae (1879–1962) and was continued well into the twentieth by men such as Erich Schmid (1907–2000). Some of them largely abandoned composition – such as Andreae and Schmid, two of the most talented composers that Switzerland has ever produced; the most extreme example was Fröhlich, who found the constraints of provincial music life so unbearable that he chose suicide instead. In Schütter's case – as Ute Stoecklin's narrative explains – his (brief) time abroad was followed first by military service, then by 30 years working backstage at the Zurich Opera House that were occasionally punctuated by choral conducting jobs outside it (often with catastrophic results). Just as with his predecessors, Schütter's compositional output now also dwindled. But when he finally left the Opera, his retirement seems to have been a catalyst for a second composing 'career', ushering in thirty years of near-uninterrupted creative activity – a fate very different from that of his earlier composing compatriots.

This late intensity of artistic endeavour on Schütter's part was only possible because he benefitted from a wide circle of friends, patrons and performers, the most significant of them being Ute Stoecklin, without whom Schütter's later *œuvre* might never have been committed to paper. Her support, performances and recordings were crucial in promoting his work, and she was also responsible for having several volumes of his songs published in the early 1990s. It was these publications that in turn brought about my own initial contact with the composer. Not long after being appointed to run the Music Department at the Zentralbibliothek Zürich in late 1990, I had come across the little book of anecdotes about him that his friend Philipp Zinsli had recently edited;[1] I found it amusing, but thought nothing more of it. A few months later, I remembered Schütter's name when I found myself cataloguing two volumes of his songs that had just been published by Musik Verlag Nepomuk, and which I found strikingly beautiful. It is the official duty of the Zurich Library to collect the works of composers active in the Canton of Zurich (which had been Schütter's home for almost half a century), and so I initiated contact, we became properly acquainted, and Schütter donated his music manuscripts to the Library on the occasion of his 85th birthday in 1995 (a friend at the Library quipped at the time that all significant artists should be convinced to give such presents on their birthdays, rather than expecting anything in the other direction).

Schütter's output is large and covers just about every genre, from opera (*Medea*) to symphony, chamber works, choruses and piano music, although it is probably his Lieder that offer the best point of entry, given that song was a prime focus of his for over 60 years (if with large gaps during his Opera House years when he composed little at all). The earliest work that Schütter later recognised is *Dumonda*, a Rumansh setting of 1931, which is clearly reminiscent of the Op. 44 songs to texts by Hermann Hesse composed in 1929 by Schütter's older compatriot Othmar Schoeck.[2] The impact that Schoeck exerted on his younger Swiss contemporaries at the time was considerable, though it was obviously the more 'Modernist' Schoeck that interested Schütter, as is especially evident in his *Serenade* for soprano and string trio of 1934. It comprises a setting of a poem by Hermann Hesse (appropriately entitled 'Three-part music') that is enclosed within two purely instrumental movements, the last of them featuring a recapitulation of music from the first. The cyclic structure and the dissonant, Neo-Classical contrapuntal textures are clearly indebted to Schoeck's *Notturno* for voice and string quartet, which had been given its Zurich premiere only a year earlier. Schoeck's mastery of form is naturally more advanced than anything to be found in the work of the young Schütter, though the latter's harmonies are overall more progressive, and it is clear that he was also keeping abreast of what the Second Viennese School was writing at the time. Schütter might have grown up in the semi-isolated alpine environment of Chur, but he is here already writing in a modernistic, Austro-German style that would have

---

[1] This was *Meinrad Schütter: Freund Meini Schütter zum 80. Wiegenfest mit herzlichen Wünschen zugeeignet vom Zinsli-Clan*, compiled by Philipp Zinsli, with drawings by his wife, the artist Verena Zinsli. Philipp Zinsli, Chur, 1990.

[2] *Dumonda* is given as a music example on pp. 46–48, above.

been familiar to anyone of the day from Berlin to Budapest and beyond. This *Serenade* deserves a place in the repertoire on its own merits; it is one of Schütter's loveliest works.

Schütter shared with Schoeck a liking for Hesse's poems, though the younger composer's taste in poetry was otherwise very different. Whereas Schoeck preferred the early German Romantics (Lenau, Eichendorff and all), Schütter's songs of the 1930s set texts by contemporary poets such as Rainer Maria Rilke, the Rumansh writer Gian Caduff and the Swiss Expressionist Karl Stamm (1890–1919), whose poetry seems to have inspired Schütter to move even further towards free atonality.[3] And all the musical influences mentioned here are already being filtered through a strong, independent artistic personality. It is remarkable that while a certain stylistic trajectory can be traced within Schütter's output – primarily in his successive abandonment of tonality – the author of these early songs is also identifiably the same composer who wrote the songs of the ensuing decades, whether *Pos o matg* of 1962, say, or the cycle *Chanzuns de la not* of 1994.

Apart from Schoeck, the contemporary Swiss music scene in the early 1930s was dominated by the generation of Neo-Classical composers born in around 1900: Willy Burkhard, Robert Blum, Paul Müller-Zürich, Conrad Beck, Adolf Brunner, Albert Moeschinger and others, some of whom had studied in France, but who all tended to adhere to a broadly Hindemithian aesthetic. Their activities were centred around the Zurich branch of the International Society for Contemporary Music (ISCM), named 'Pro Musica', which they founded in 1935.[4] They were also all members of the Swiss Musicians' Association (hereinafter SMA), which had a much broader base and was still conservative in outlook. Its President from 1931 to 1941 was Carl Vogler, a late-Romantic composer concurrently the Director of the Zurich Conservatoire and an immensely powerful figure in Swiss music. His intense, personal dislike of Schütter[5] had serious consequences for the younger man. After excluding the young Schütter from the Conservatoire, Vogler similarly banned him from membership of the SMA, thereby ostracising him from the most important music organisation in the country and effectively barring his music from its concerts. Schütter's works of the 1930s would not have been out of place in the Zurich Pro Musica. But he was a decade younger than Burkhard, Blum and Co., as yet unknown and unestablished, unable to complete his studies for lack of money, and his prime concern for the moment

---

[3] Discussed on p. 48, above.
[4] Joseph Willimann, *Pro Musica. Der neuen Musik zulieb. 50 Jahre Pro Musica. Ortsgruppe Zürich der Internationalen Gesellschaft für Neue Musik (IGNM)*, Atlantis Musikbuch-Verlag, Zurich, 1988.
[5] Discussed on pp. 41–44, above.

was getting enough work to be able to live. And then the War intervened anyway, necessitating military service in the far south of the country. Since the SMA became the Swiss national section of the ISCM in 1946, Schütter's exclusion from the former meant that he never became established in the latter either, and his post-War employment at the Opera House left little time for composing anything at all. What's more, the post-War period saw both the SMA and the local ISCM increasingly dominated by a new generation whose idol was Webern and whose chosen aesthetic was serial. As a composer, Schütter was proving adept at falling between many stools.

It was nevertheless typical of his dogged nature that he recognised what he lacked, and took active steps to remedy the situation – hence his initiating a composition course by correspondence with Willy Burkhard in 1941 (one of the above-mentioned Swiss Hindemithians) and his enrolment to study with the master himself a decade later when Hindemith was appointed professor at Zurich University.[6] It is a little ironic that it was only in the early 1950s that Hindemith's influence became obvious in Schütter's music, some twenty years after most of his older Swiss Neo-Classical colleagues had succumbed, and at a time when his younger colleagues were becoming post-Webernians. The Piano Sonatina of 1955 is a prime example. Its austere, two-part counterpoint, preponderance of fifths in the harmony and use of canon are all highly reminiscent of Hindemith (Ex. 4). There are traces of his influence, too, in the opera *Medea* that Schütter reworked in 1952 (its use of 'traditional' numbers naturally places it in a Neo-Classical orbit), but the direct impact of Hindemith soon disappears from his music, and Schütter's works of the 1950s and early 1960s suggest an endeavour to unite the neo-modal Neo-Classicism of Hindemith with the atonal, expressive possibilities of the Second Viennese School. In this regard, Schütter's recollection of the world premiere of Schoenberg's *Moses und Aron* in Zurich in 1957 is fascinating. When he writes of how Hindemith stood apart afterwards, visibly moved, Schütter is probably projecting his own feelings onto the man he admired: it was Schütter who was overwhelmed by the performance, and who felt a need to reconcile the two aesthetic worlds in which he was at home.

However much Schütter's work at the Zurich Opera House might have held him back as a composer, there is no doubt that it enabled him to experience all manner of music at first hand. The Zurich Opera was still very much a 'provincial' house when compared with the big German cities, but it was usually the first Swiss venue for the latest operas from abroad, ranging from Britten's *Peter Grimes* to Gershwin's *Porgy and Bess*, Stravinsky's *The Rake's Progress* and, of course, *Moses und Aron*. Schütter

[6] Discussed on pp. 67–71, above.

Ex. 4

was also an avid concert-goer who delighted in hearing the latest music, however modern and avant-garde. Unlike many of his older colleagues, old age for him brought no lapse into conservatism. It should not surprise anyone that he simply took up his composing career again as soon as his everyday duties diminished, but what is surprising is his late interest in all manner of contemporary techniques, from serialism to Fibonacci rows and even multiphonics (as in the first page of his *Four Pieces for Solo Clarinet*, given in Ex. 5). Besides a wealth of new songs, chamber works and piano music, these late years also brought forth his longest instrumental work – and in my opinion his most significant – namely the Piano Concerto, first performed by Tomás Kramreiter in 1985. Its 'programme' is forest dieback – which in the mid-1980s had become a matter of real concern in the alpine region, and to which Schütter felt moved to respond. But this is no political work raging against abstract ecological wrongs. Instead, Schütter evokes his own, personal reminiscences of the forests of his childhood outside Chur, which gives the work a real emotional impact.

Ex. 5

On paper, the Piano Concerto is densely polyphonic, atonal, even well-nigh athematic, and seems somehow breathless, with almost every *forte* soon giving way to a *piano*, and frequent pauses interrupting the flow. But hearing it reveals the presence of a clear harmonic and quasi-dramatic trajectory. Its textures are transparent, and its motivic connections become perceptible to the ear in a way that is not immediately obvious on the page. And the Brahms quotation towards the end of the second movement is hinted at so subtly in advance that when it comes, it sounds like a distant memory (which in a sense, I suppose, it already is).

Where the Piano Concerto skilfully uses the fragmentary and the aphoristic almost as stylistic devices, they become increasingly dominant in many of Schütter's later works, such as the String Quartet and, especially, in his Symphony, which he completed at the age of 89. At times in the Symphony in particular, it seems as if fragments of material are all that remain of a work over which he had laboured intermittently for 60 years. One is here reminded of Adorno's view of 'late style' in Beethoven, in which,

> Touched by death, the hand of the master sets free the masses of material that he used to form; its tears and fissures, witnesses to the finite powerlessness of the I confronted with Being, are its final work. [...] And

as splinters, fallen away and abandoned, they themselves finally revert to expression [...].[7]

Such an interpretation would seem to have been confirmed by Schütter himself, when he told Michael Eidenbenz of his symphony that "'The opening material regrettably doesn't appear again later" [...] as if what he had created had somehow eluded his control and taken on a life of its own during the creative process'.[8] And yet one should exercise caution in assuming any gradual lack of control over the material in Schütter's last works, for there are some – such as the Piano Trio of 1996, which sounds remarkably youthful and even plays with allusions to popular music – that seem to confirm, conversely, that Schütter still knew exactly what he wanted to compose and was perfectly capable of delivering it.

Perhaps the oddest conundrum about Schütter the composer is how he managed to stay unacknowledged in Switzerland for so long. To be sure, he was for a long time actively excluded from the local musical fraternity and in any case adhered to an aesthetic that in the era of Darmstadt was hardly up to date. But it is still strange, as Peter Palmer remarked of Schütter, that in the Zurich of the early 1960s, 'nobody at that time – and least of all the man himself – suggested that here was a creative artist of stature'.[9] The standard reference works for Swiss music ignored him completely. He is absent from the volume *40 contemporary swiss composers* of 1956,[10] from the Swiss Musicians' Dictionary of 1964,[11] and even from all three editions of *Swiss Contemporary Composers*, the final edition of which, published in 1993, proudly announced that it included all the composers from the previous editions and had added even more, making a grand total of 191.[12] But still without Schütter. He does not even figure in the follow-up volume *Swiss Choral Composers* of 1999, despite having long composed two masses and a plethora of smaller choral works.[13]

Philipp Zinsli's little book of Schütter anecdotes offers an inkling of what to my mind was a major reason for Schütter's long lack of recognition in his native land. He was immensely funny. Far funnier than any of those written anecdotes suggest, for the printed word is unable to convey his

[7] Theodor W. Adorno, trans. Susan H. Gillespie: 'Late Style in Beethoven', in Adorno, *Essays on Music*, ed. Richard Leppert, University of California Press, Berkeley, 2002, pp. 564–568, here 566.
[8] Discussed on p. 122, above.
[9] Palmer, *loc. cit.* (2001), p. 56.
[10] Swiss Composers' League, *40 contemporary swiss composers. 40 compositores suizos contemporáneos*, Bodensee-Verlag, Amriswil, 1956.
[11] Willi Schuh, Hans Ehinger, Pierre Meylan and Hans Peter Schanzlin, *Schweizer Musiker-Lexikon. Dictionnaire des musiciens suisses 1964*, Atlantis Verlag, Zurich, 1964.
[12] SUISA-Stiftung für Musik, *Schweizer Komponisten unserer Zeit*, 3rd edn., Amadeus Verlag, Winterthur, 1993.
[13] SUISA-Stiftung für Musik, *Schweizer Chor-Komponisten*, Hug Musikverlage, Zurich, 1999.

exquisite sense of comic timing and the theatricality of his presence (something that he had no doubt honed over the many years of his daily work in the theatre itself). So funny, in fact, that I think it was decidedly to his detriment in the serious, Zwinglian atmosphere of post-War Zurich. His humour was neither particularly intellectual, nor was it vulgar (for my part, I cannot recall him ever uttering profanities, though I don't remember him ever objecting to them either). Nor was there anything of the slapstick about him – though his gait admittedly had something of the fluidity of Monsieur Hulot in Jacques Tati's *Playtime*. He was a master of seemingly improvised, wry wit, delivered with at most a slight smile and in a measured, rolling accent the like of which I've never heard before or since. Once, after a performance in Chur that Schütter attended, he joined the members of our ensemble for post-concert drinks in the bar of our hotel. He sat more or less silent for a long time, and since he was already 85, we all assumed that he was simply tired, and felt a little sorry for him. But during a momentary hiatus in the conversation, Schütter clearly decided he'd been silent long enough, so with a grand *non sequitur* about how his father had once 'helped to run over the first dog in Chur', he got everyone's attention and then embarked on a long, hilarious, rambling, semi-autobiographical narrative that seemed spontaneous, but that in retrospect was skilfully structured. The previously uncommunicative octogenarian wasn't tired at all, but possessed of apparently inexhaustible energy, and from then on until the moment the rest of us went to bed (we were on average over fifty years his junior), he had our undivided attention. In another life, he would have been a star at High Table in any Cambridge college. But the Swiss – while far from humourless[14] – have always preferred to compartmentalise their gifts, and to judge from my many conversations with Swiss colleagues, it was widely assumed that someone as funny as Schütter couldn't possibly be a serious composer, and that a man given to witty, off-the cuff aphorisms couldn't be capable of constructing large-scale musical forms. But he was actually adept at both. It is not surprising that recordings of Schütter's music have over the past 25 years received better, more frequent reviews in the English-speaking press than in his homeland. Perhaps the publication of this book about him in English will help to convince his compatriots that he was truly a composer of stature after all.

---

[14] The author is today Swiss himself, and wouldn't want to be anything else.

Catalogue of Works

The manuscripts of Schütter's compositions (and the composer's own amended manuscript copies) are held today by the Zentralbibliothek Zürich under the shelfmark 'Mus NL 2'. The catalogue of this archive, by Carlos Chanfón, Andrea Barblan and Angelika Salge, is available online via the library's website at https://zbcollections.ch/home. Durations of works and the dates and venues of first performances are given here where these are known.

Abbreviations
Performing forces
pic – piccolo; fl – flute; ob – oboe; cor angl – cor anglais; cl – clarinet; bcl – bass clarinet; bn – bassoon; cbn – contrabassoon; hn – horn; tpt – trumpet; trbn – trombone; tb – tuba; timp – timpani; perc – percussion; hp – harp; org – organ; pf – piano; cel – celeste; vn – violin; va – viola; vc – cello; db – double bass; str – strings

Other abbreviations
FP – first performance
Instr. – instrumentation
Publ. – publication

Operas
Medea
Opera in three acts
Libretto by Meinrad Schütter after Franz Grillparzer, Euripides, Apollonius Rhodius and Jean Anouilh 1941 (first version), rev. 1957; in 2005, Ute Stoecklin and Peter Niklaus Steiner (under the composer's guidance) made a shortened version for four voices, speaker and piano
Dramatis personae:
Kreon, King of Corinth – bass
Kreusa, his daughter – soprano
Jason – tenor
Medea – mezzo-soprano
Gora, Medea's nurse – soprano
A herald – baritone
Aigeus, King of Athens – baritone
Leader of the chorus (speaking role)
A slave, the two sons of Jason and Medea, the followers of the Herald, the Mýstēs
Date and place: Greece, Antiquity

Instr.: 3 fl (3 also pic), 3 ob (3 also cor angl), 3 cl (3 also bcl), 3 bn (3 also cbn) – 4 hn, 3 tpt, 3 trbn, tb – timp, perc – hp – str – pf, cel
Duration: 2 hours 30'; abridged version: 55'
FP (of the abridged version with piano accompaniment): 1 November 2005 in the Museum der Kulturen in Basel

Die Flüchtlinge
Opera in four acts by Alfred Schlenker (1876–1950) to a libretto by Hermann Hesse, arranged and abridged by Meinrad Schütter, Werner Kaegi and Hans Reinhart as an opera in three acts.
Original version: 1910–40?; revised version by Schütter, Kaegi and Reinhart: 1951–54?
    It seems that the original was never orchestrated, but exists only in a draft with piano accompaniment. The revision by Schütter & Co. is similarly only for voices and piano.
Dramatis personae (revised version):
Count Riccardo – bass-baritone
Giulietta, Riccardo's daughter – soprano
Count Angelo Castelnuovo, first a novice monk, then a knight – baritone
Tommaso, a young monk – tenor
The prior of the monastery – bass
Clarissa, Giulietta's foster sister and confidante – high soprano
Riccardo's main servant – baritone
Monks, servants, the Count's hunters, people

Rübezahl
A Christmas tale by Rolf Frickart
1980
Incomplete; only a version for piano solo exists.

Ballets
Dr Joggeli sött go Birli schüttle
Ballet for children (eight dancers), two pianos and percussion, after the picture book by Lisa Wenger
1950–51, revised 1991
Dramatis personae:
Der Joggeli
Das Hündchen
Der Stecken
Das Feuer
Das Wasser
Das Kälbchen
Der Metzger
Der Meister
Duration: 20'

FP: 1951 in Zurich. Members of the Mario Volkart Dance School. Meinrad Schütter and Alfred Zäch (pianos)

Clownesque
A pantomime for one dancer and piano
1995
Duration: 3′

Orchestral Works
Fünf Varianten und Metamorphose
For chamber orchestra
1939, rev. 1949
Instr.: fl, ob, cl, bn – 2 hn, tpt – timp – str
Duration: 10′
Publ.: Sordino SEM 0539
FP: (version 1) 30 March 1939 in Zurich. Zurich Chamber Orchestra, cond. Alexander Schaichet; (version 2) 7 January 1946 in the Zurich Radio Studio. Beromünster Radio Orchestra, cond. Hermann Scherchen

Symphony in One Movement
1939, rev. 1965, 1970, 1999
Instr.: 2 fl, 2 ob, 2 cl, 2 bn – 4 hn, 2 tpt, 2 trbn – timp – hp – str
Duration: 16′
Publ.: IDEM-Rutz
FP: 22 September 2000 in Chur. Orchesterverein Chur, cond. Luzius Müller

Ricercare No. 1
1946, rev. 1952, 1956
Instr.: 2 fl, 2 ob, 2 cl, 2 bn – 4 hn, 2 tpt, 2 trbn – timp – str
Duration: 4′30″
FP: 11 March 1946 (?) in the Zurich Radio Studio. Beromünster Radio Orchestra, cond. Hermann Scherchen
Note: This work was originally performed under the title *Fuge*. An archive recording of Scherchen's performance on the radio is held by the Zentralbibliothek Zürich, shelfmark: Ton F 3229

Suite for Small Orchestra
1955
Instr.: fl, 2 cl, bn – 2 hn, tpt – timp – str
Duration: 7′
FP: 1960 in Chur. Winterthur City Orchestra, cond. Ernst Schweri Jr

March No. 1
1974
Instr.: 2 fl, 2 ob, 2 cl, 2 bn – 2 hn, 2 tpt, 3 trbn – timp, perc – str
Duration: 4′
FP: 13 October 1974, Zurich Radio Orchestra, cond. Hans Möckel

Metamorphosis
For string orchestra
1975, rev. 1988
Duration 5′
FP: 29 July 1988 in La Tour de Peilz. Ensemble Miramis, cond. Thomas Gartmann

Concentus
For string orchestra
1981
Duration: 3′
FP: 18 February 1990 in Seattle (USA). Northwest Chamber Orchestra, cond.
Eric Shumsky

Pastorale I. Adorazione dei pastori II
For string orchestra
1988
Duration: 3′
FP: 11 November 1995 in Witikon. Kirchgemeinde-Orchester Witikon, cond. Chris
Walton

Pastorale III. Adorazione dei pastori IV
For string orchestra
1988
Duration: 4′30″
FP: 16 February 1990 in Seattle (USA). Northwest Chamber Orchestra, cond.
Eric Shumsky

March No. 2
1990
Instr.: fl, cl – tpt – timp – str – pf
Duration: 4′
Dedication: To Brigitte Barandun and Rahman Bahman on the occasion of their
wedding

Concertos
Duo Concertante 'Quasi una Fantasia'
For violin, viola and orchestra
1966
Instr.: 2 fl, 2 ob, 2 cl, 2 bn – 4 hn, 2 tpt, 2 trbn, tb – timp – str
Duration: 17′
FP: 2 April 1967 in Chur. Bodensee-Sinfonie Orchester, cond. Ernst Schweri Jr

Piano Concerto
For piano and string orchestra
1985
Duration: 25′
Publ.: Sordino ediziuns musicalas

FP: 13 May 1986 in Zurich. Tomás Kramreiter (piano), Zurich Chamber Orchestra cond. Christof Escher
Dedication: To Tomás Kramreiter
Recording: *Schütter, Schaeuble: Klavierkonzerte*, Musikszene Schweiz/Migros-Genossenschafts-Bund MGB CD 6162 (2000)

Pastorale II. Adorazione dei pastori III
For clarinet and string orchestra
Duration: 11′
FP: 16 February 1990 in Seattle (USA). Northwest Chamber Orchestra, cond. Eric Shumsky
Recording: *Schütter, Schaeuble: Klavierkonzerte*, Musikszene Schweiz/Migros-Genossenschafts-Bund MGB CD 6162 (2000)

Chamber Music and Works for Solo Strings or Winds
Serenade
For flute, oboe and clarinet
1934, rev. 1987
Duration: 2′30″
FP: 28 July 1983 in Obersaxen at the International Summer Festival

Two Pieces
For cello and piano
1935
Duration: 15′
Publ.: Musikverlag Nepomuk (Aarau) MN 9945
FP: 5 August 1982 in Lenzerheide. Luzius Gartmann (cello) and Russel Ryan (piano)

Phantasie
For oboe d'amore and piano
1936
Duration: 5′
FP: 8 November 1983 in Chur. Lukas Meuli (oboe d'amore) and Reto Fritz (piano)

First Suite
For clarinet and piano
1939, rev. 1955
Duration: 10′
FP: 1967 in Zurich. Hansjürg Leuthold (clarinet) and Dorothea Isler (piano)
Recording: *Meinrad Schütter: Kammermusik und instrumental begleitete Gesänge 1939–1998*, swiss pan 510 316 (2000)

Verbunkos (Chanson et danse hongroise)
For violin and piano
1957
Duration: 4′

FP: 20 September 1990 in Küsnacht. Suzanne Leon (violin) and Anne de Dadelsen
(piano)

Invention I
For two clarinets in B flat
1969
Duration: 1′

Invention II
For oboe and two clarinets in B flat
1969
Duration: 1′

Widmung
For two violins and viola
1969
Duration: 1′30″

*Clavis Astartis magica I. Metamorphosis, after a series of notes from the opera
'Faust' by Ferruccio Busoni*
For violin and piano
1973
Duration: 6′
FP: 11 May 1989 in Paris. Suzanne Leon (violin) and Stephanie Leon (piano)
Recording: *Meinrad Schütter: Kammermusik und instrumental begleitete Gesänge
1939–1998*, Swisspan 510 316 (2000)

Clavis Astartis magica II
For violin solo
1973 rev. 1995
Duration: 5′30″
Publ.: Musikverlag Müller & Schade (Bern) M&S 1710
FP: 21 May 1986 in Bern. Alexander Wijnkoop (violin)

Herbei, oh ihr Gläubigen
For violin, clarinet and organ
1979
Duration: 3′

Suite
For cello solo
1979
Duration: 11′
Publ.: Musikverlag Nepomuk MN 12058
FP: 18 November 1983 in the Konzertstudio Chur. Kai Scheffler (cello)

Ricercare No. 2
For oboe, clarinet, horn and bassoon
1983

Duration: 2'
FP: 28 July 1983 in Obersaxen at the International Summer Festival. Performers unknown

Second Suite
For clarinet and piano
1984?
Duration: 14'
FP: 17 December 1986 in Zurich. René Oswald (clarinet) and Annette Weisbrod (piano)

Antiquarisch
For two clarinets and bassoon
1984–85
Duration: 1'30"

Kanon (Spruch)
For violin and clarinet
1985
Duration: 1'

Sonata for Cello and Piano
1985
Duration: 10'
Dedication: 'To Ruth Barandun'
FP: no date established, in Chur. Christoph Cajöri (cello) and Meinrad Schütter (piano)

Wind Octet
For flute, oboe, three clarinets, two bassoons and horn
1985
Duration: 13'
FP: 25 July 1983 in Obersaxen at the International Summer Festival. Performers unknown

Nachtstücke I und II (Spiegelungen)
1986 rev. 1996
For flute, clarinet, piano/harpsichord
Duration: 4'
FP: 2 June 1987 in Domat/Ems. René Oswald (clarinet), Mario Giovanoli (flute) and Meinrad Schütter (piano)

Four Pieces for Clarinet
1983, revised 1987
Duration: 10'
Publ. (revised version): Musikverlag Nepomuk MN 9596
FP: 17 March 1983 in Lenzerheide; revised version 23 July 1987 in Zurich – both by René Oswald (clarinet)

Metamorphosis II
For string quartet
1988
Duration: 4'30"
FP: 26 March 2000 in Küsnacht. Aurora Quartet: Ardina Nehring, Brigitta Barandun (violins), Astrid Leuthold (viola), Ursula Baumann (cello)

Notturno
For violin and piano
1988
Duration: 4'40"
Publ. Musikverlag Nepomuk MN 9477
FP: 20 September 1990 in Küsnacht. Suzanne Leon (violin) and Anne de Dadelsen (piano)

Humoreske (Hommage à Francis Poulenc)
For clarinet and piano
1989
Duration: 5'
Publ.: Musikverlag Nepomuk MN 9595
FP: 27 May 1989 in Domat/Ems. René Oswald (clarinet) and Meinrad Schütter (piano)
NB: also available in a version for viola and piano

String Quartet
1990
Duration: 14'
FP: 10 February 2019 in Basel. Ensemble Aventure: Friedmann Treiber, Felix Treiber (violins), Silvie Altenburger (viola), Beverly Ellis (cello)
Recording: *20th Century Swiss String Quartets*, Guild Music GMCD 7254 (2006)

Trio for three clarinets (or basset horns)
1992
Duration: 11'
Publ.: Musikverlag Gottfried Aegler (CH-Erlenbach)
FP: 19 June 1993 in Chur. Calamus Trio (Josias Just, Martin Imfeld, Martin Zimmermann)
Recording: *Meinrad Schütter: Kammermusik und instrumental begleitete Gesänge 1939–1998*, swiss pan 510 316
Note: Also exists in an arrangement by Hans Martin Ulbrich for clarinet, cor anglais and bassoon, published by Musikverlag Müller & Schade M&S 2293

Invention III
For flute and piano
1993
Duration: 3'
Publ. Musikverlag Müller & Schade MN 2351
FP: 21 August 1993 in Basel. Fränzi Badertscher (flute) and Ute Stoecklin (piano)

Invention IV
For clarinet and piano
1993
Duration: 3′
FP: 19 September 1993 in Chur. René Oswald (clarinet) and Ute Stoecklin (piano)

Romance
For horn and piano
1993, rev. 2001
Duration: 2′
Publ.: Musikverlag Müller & Schade M&S 2352

Bagatelle
For horn and piano
1993–95
Duration: 2′
Publ.: Musikverlag Müller & Schade M&S 2353
FP: 24 July 2002 in Museo Archeologico di Aosta. Martin Roos (horn) and Andrea
Maggiora (piano)

Herbei, oh ihr Gläubigen
For clarinet and organ
1994
Duration: 2′

Consolazione
For clarinet and organ
1995
Duration: 7′
FP: 9 June 1995 in Chur. Martin Imfeld (clarinet) and Meinrad Schütter (organ)

Trio in One Movement
For violin, cello and piano
1996
Duration: 8′
Publ.: Musikverlag Müller & Schade M&S 2353
FP: 4 October 1998 in Villeneuve (Canton Vaud). Fennica Trio: Helena Maffli-
Nissinen (piano), Dorota Sosnowska (violin), Jarmo Vainio (cello)
Recording: *Meinrad Schütter: Kammermusik und instrumental begleitete Gesänge
1939–1998*, Swisspan 510 316 (2000)

Kinderlied
For trumpet and piano
1997
Duration: 2′

Poema
For flute and piano
1997

Duration: 4′
Publ.: Musikverlag Nepomuk MN 12032
FP: 24 January 1999 in Basel. Carsten Hustedt (flute) and Ute Stoecklin (piano)
Recording: *Meinrad Schütter: Kammermusik und instrumental begleitete Gesänge 1939–1998*, Swisspan 510 316 (2000)

Duo for Flute and Cello, after a scene in Aristophanes' *Frogs*
1998
Duration: 7′
Publ. Musikverlag Müller & Schade M&S 2170
FP: 26 November 1998 in Vilnius. Carsten Hustedt (flute) and Käthi Gohl (cello)
Recording: *Meinrad Schütter: Kammermusik und instrumental begleitete Gesänge 1939–1998*, Swisspan 510 316 (2000)

Piece for cello and piano
1998
Duration: 4′30″
Publ.: Musikverlag Nepomuk MN 12031
FP: 24 January 1999, Basel. Jarmo Vainio (cello) and Ute Stoecklin (piano)

Gommer Suite (Dix miniatures valaisannes)
For flute, violin and viola
1999
Duration: 10′
Publ. Musikverlag Müller & Schade M&S 2354
FP: 20 July 1999 in Niederwald (Switzerland). Trio Diletto Musicale (Bonn): Klaus Bleidorn (flute), Gisela Lehmacher (violin) and Hans Georg Büchel (viola)

Separate Einbildungen
For clarinet, violin, cello and piano
1999
Duration: 10′
FP: 12 June 1999 in Biała Podlaska (Poland). Romuald Gołębiowski (clarinet), Dorota Sosnowska (violin), Jarmo Vainio (cello), Helena Maffli-Nissinen (piano)
Note: title in Polish *Odrebne Fickje*. With underlaid texts by Stanisław Jerzy Lec from his *Myśli nieuczesane*.

Promenades à Mannheim
Six pieces for solo flute
2001
Duration: 7′
Publ.: Musikverlag Nepomuk MN 12038 (Nos. 1–3), 12039 (Nos. 4–6)
Note: '1–3 avec Stamitz, 4–6 avec Mozart'. These six pieces were initially conceived as cadenzas for each movement of the flute concertos in G major, Op. 29, by Carl Stamitz and in G major, K313 (285c) by Mozart, but may be played as an independent suite.

FP (as a suite for solo flute): 27 July 2001 in the Church of St Aurelius at the Klosterfestspiele in Hirsau (Germany). Carsten Hustedt (flute)

FP (as cadenzas): Nos. 1–3 in Stamitz Concerto, Op. 29, on 12 February 2001 in the Stadtkirche Leonberg, Stuttgart. Carsten Hustedt (flute), St Christopher Chamber Orchestra of Vilnius, cond. Donatus Katkus

Recording: *Spiritoso!*, RBM Musikproduktion 463042/43 (double album; 2006)

Fanfares
For three trumpets, two horns, tenor trombone and timpani
2004
Duration: 15′
FP: 23 October 2004 in the Congress House, Lucerne

Quartet
For oboe, trumpet, bassoon and cello
2005
Duration: 10′
Publ.: Musikverlag Nepomuk MN 12052
FP: 2 October 2005 in the Seehof, Küsnacht. Roman Schmid (oboe), Thomas Portmann (trumpet), Urs Dengler (bassoon), Anne Christine Vandevalle (cello)

Suite
For solo flute
2005
Duration: 5′
Publ.: Müller & Schade M&S 2351
FP: 25 October 2005 at the University of Pretoria (South Africa). Cobus du Toit (flute)

Organ Works
Antienne du chant grigorien
1982
Duration: 2′30″

Adorazione dei Pastori
1991
Duration: 3′
Publ.: Sinus 10001
FP: 17 February 1993 in Mumbai (India). Albert Bolliger
Recording: *Christ Ascended: Swiss Religious Music of the 20th Century*, Guild Music GMCG 7177 (1999)

Partita: 'Mit meinem Gott geh' ich zur Ruh'
1992
Duration: 4′
Publ.: Sinus 10001
FP: 17 February 1993 in Mumbai. Albert Bolliger

Recording: *Christ Ascended: Swiss Religious Music of the 20th Century*, Guild Music GMCG 7177 (1999)

Postludium
1992
Duration: 2'30"

Meditation
2001
Duration: 4'
FP: 5 September 2002 at the University of Pretoria (South Africa). Janandi van Schoor

De Leonardo Pisano
2001
Duration: 7'
FP: 5 September 2002 at the University of Pretoria (South Africa). Hannes Ebersohn

Novellette
2004
Duration: 5'
Note: after the story 'The Goat of Mr Seguin' by Alphonse Daudet

Piano Duets and Duos
Verbunkos
For piano duet
1957, rev. 1990
Duration: 4'
FP: 16 August 1975 in Chur. Sara Novikoff and Meinrad Schütter

Introduzione e Passacaglia from the ballet Dr Joggeli sött go Birli schüttle
For two pianos
Arranged in 1986
FP: 20 February 1986 in Basel. Susanne Stoecklin and Ute Stoecklin

Foxtrott, collage d'après 'Les enfants et les Sortilèges' de M. Ravel et un noël
For piano duet
1988/1993
Duration: 2'30"
FP: 21 December 1993 in Basel. Meinrad Schütter and Ute Stoecklin

Piano Solo
Four Small Pieces
1933/1960
I.   Hommage à Paul Hindemith
II. Hommage à Paul Hindemith
III. Kinderreigen im Hinterhof

IV. Regentag im Schrebergarten
Duration: 4′
Publ.: Musikverlag Müller & Schade M&S 2350
FP: 1938 in Chur. Alfred Zäch (piano)
Note: There were originally five pieces, the fifth being 'Petite scène alpestre', which was removed before the first performance of the set in 1938 but survives in Schütter's archive in the Zentralbibliothek Zürich.
Radio recording: https://neo.mx3.ch/meisch. Rudolf Ambach (piano). This recording, made on 6 July 1978 in the Zurich Radio Studio, includes the original fifth piece, here given as 'Scène alpèstre'.

Passacaglia
1933/1973
Duration: 2′
Radio recording: https://neo.mx3.ch/meisch. Rudolf Ambach (piano). Made on 6 July 1978 at the Zurich Radio Studio.

Sonata
1934/1954
Duration: 13′30″
Publ.: Musikverlag Müller & Schade M&S 2350
FP: Date unknown. Radio Beromünster (Zurich). Rudolf Ambach
Radio recording: https://neo.mx3.ch/meisch. Rudolf Ambach (piano). Made on 22 September 1972 at the Zurich Radio Studio.

Präludium und Postludium
1936/1975/1993
Duration: 5′30″
Publ. (only *Präludium*): Musikverlag Müller & Schade, Bern, M&S 2350
FP: Date unknown. Radio Beromünster (Zurich). Rudolf Ambach
Radio recording: https://neo.mx3.ch/meisch. Rudolf Ambach (piano). Made on 6 July 1978 at the Zurich Radio Studio.

Six Variations on the Portuguese Christmas Carol 'Adeste fideles'
1939
Duration: 10′
FP: 17 December 1986 in Chur. Meinrad Schütter
Radio recording: https://neo.mx3.ch/meisch. Rudolf Ambach (piano). Made on 22 September 1972 at the Zurich Radio Studio.

Sonatina
1939/1955
Duration: 6′
Publ.: Musikverlag Nepomuk MN 9475
FP: Date unknown (1972?). Radio Beromünster (Zurich). Rudolf Ambach
Radio recording: https://neo.mx3.ch/meisch. Rudolf Ambach (piano). Made on 22 September 1972 at the Zurich Radio Studio.

Tanzstück
1957
Duration: 2′

Albumblatt
1970
Duration: 1′

Fugue
1971
Duration: 1′

Nachmittag eines Clavizimbels
1973
Duration: 3′

Praeludium
1980
Duration: 1′

Five Little Variations on a Children's Song
1980
Duration: 2′30″
Publ.: Musikverlag Nepomuk MN 12045
FP: 18 September 1993 in Chur. Ute Stoecklin

Five Persian Songs and Dances
1981
Duration: 9′
Publ.: Musikverlag Müller & Schade M&S 2350
FP: 25 May 1987 in Zurich. Sara Novikoff

Variations on a Rhythm
1982
Duration: 4′30″
Publ.: Musikverlag Müller & Schade M&S 2350
FP: 26 January 1983 in Zurich. Tomás Kramreiter

Raumspielmusik
1985
Duration: 5′

Musik für Klavier in einer 'Nicht-nicht-Form'
1987
Duration: 5′

Churer Legende von Spukgeistern und Spiegeleien
1988
Duration: 5′
FP: 18 September 1993 in Chur. Ute Stoecklin

Four Piano Pieces
1989
1. Auf ein altes Bild
2. Study
3. Tanz der Spukgeister im Scaläratobel
4. '... oder wie die Zeit vergeht'
Publ.: Musikverlag Nepomuk MN 9476
FP: 26 May 1990 in Basel. Ute Stoecklin

Ricercare No. 3
1991
Duration: 2'

Canto ermetico
1991
Duration: 3'30"
Publ.: Musikverlag Müller & Schade M&S 2350
FP: 20 September 1995 in the Konzertstudio in Chur. Ute Stoecklin

Anagramm
1993
Duration: 3'
Publ.: Musikverlag Müller & Schade M&S 2350
FP: 20 September 1995 in the Konzertstudio in Chur. Ute Stoecklin

Clownesque
1995
> Ballets

Portugiesische Weihnacht
1996
Duration: 2'

Bernadetten-Lieder: Six miniatures for piano
1998
Duration: 5'
Publ.: Musikverlag Nepomuk MN 12045
FP: 2 October 2005 in the Seehof, Küsnacht. Ute Stoecklin

Jul-Lied für Kaya
2000
Duration: 40"
Publ.: Musikverlag Nepomuk MN 12045

Monsieur Fibonacci fait ses compliments pour le cinquième anniversaire de Mlle Kaya
2001
Duration: 1'
Publ.: Musikverlag Nepomuk MN 12045

Choral Works with Accompaniment
Grosse Messe
For mixed chorus, soloists and organ
1939/1950/1970
Duration: 38′
Publ.: Musikverlag Müller & Schade M&S 2212
FP: 25 January 1981 in Chur. Kammerchor Chur, cond. Lucius Juon. Martin Derungs (organ), Helen Keller, Brigitte Kuhn (sopranos), Kale Lani Okazaki (contralto), Kurt Huber (tenor), Michel Brodard (bass-baritone)
Recording: *Bap Nos. In memoriam Meinrad Schütter*, Guild Music GMCD 7349 (2010)

Wanderers Nachtlied (Johann Wolfgang von Goethe)
For men's chorus and large orchestra
1948 (?)
Duration: 3′20″

Liebe leidet nicht, Gesellen (Johann Wolfgang von Goethe)
For men's chorus and organ
1967, rev. 1977
Duration: 4′

Da geht der Zug der Brüder (Martin Schmid)
For mixed chorus and guitar
1975
Duration: 3′

Herbei, oh ihr Gläubigen (Adeste Fideles)
For chorus, oboe and string orchestra
1978, rev. 1992
Duration: 4′30″

Neujahr (Max Mumenthaler)
For women's chorus and guitar
1978
Duration: 2′30″

Porcorum causa (Albert Vigoleis Thelen)
For men's chorus and piano
1982
Duration: 2′30″

Lied der Flösser II (Urs Martin Strub)
For men's chorus and piano
1983
Duration: 3′

5 Variations on 'Macht hoch die Tür'
For solo soprano, chorus, flute, trumpet, brass or organ
1985

Morgen (Gottfried Keller)
For men's chorus and piano
1986
Duration: 4'30"

Kleine Messe
For soprano, contralto, women's chorus and organ
1989
Duration: 16'
FP: 2 May 1989 in St Otmar's Church in St Gallen. Verena Ehrler (soprano),
Beatrice Hoby (contralto), Flavio Dora (organ)

Adorazione dei pastori
For chorus, flute and string orchestra
1992
Duration: 3'

Lied der Flösser IV (Urs Martin Strub)
For men's chorus, clarinet and string orchestra
1992
Duration: 5'

Chor seliger Knaben heiliger Anachoreten (Pater Seraphicus) from *Faust II* (Johann
Wolfgang von Goethe)
For chorus and chamber orchestra
1993
Instr.: fl, cl, hn, str
Duration: 3'

Pascas (Ser Mattli Conrad)
For chorus, flute and string orchestra
1993
Duration: 4'30"

Choral Works *a cappella*
Choral I, 'Mit meinem Gott geh ich zur Ruh'
For mixed chorus
1940
Duration: 3'

Choral II, 'Ach komm füll unsere Seelen ganz'
For mixed chorus
1943
Duration: 3'

Ögls e stailas (Men Rauch)
For men's chorus
1953
Duration: 2'
FP: 1 April 2005 in the Gallery Maison 44, Basel (with four solo voices). Schubert Quartet, Zurich (Frédéric Gindraux, Tino Brütsch, tenors; Samuel Zünd, baritone; Michael Leibundgut, bass)

Zuspruch (Nandor Währing)
For mixed chorus
1953
Duration: 3'

Ach Mutter, gib mir keinen Mann (anon.)
For women's chorus
1954
Note: An arrangement of the song by Jobst van Brandt (1517–70). No. 2 of *Chorsätze für Frauenstimmen*

Hymnus 'Tantum ergo' (Thomas Aquinus)
For mixed chorus
1954
Duration: 3'
Publ.: H. Hindermann

Zwischen Berg und tiefem Tal (trad.)
For women's chorus
1954
Duration: 1'
Note: An arrangement of the traditional song. No. 1 of *Chorsätze für Frauenstimmen*

Offertorium 'Ad ducam eos'
For mixed chorus
1962
Duration: 2'
Publ.: Musikverlag Müller & Schade M&S 977

Trost (Nandor Währing)
For women's chorus
1964
Duration: 1'30"

Schwere Nacht (Adolf Frey)
1973 (?)
For men's chorus
Duration: 3'

FP: 1 April 2005 in the Gallery Maison 44, Basel (with four solo voices). Schubert Quartet, Zurich (Frédéric Gindraux, Tino Brütsch, tenors; Samuel Zünd, baritone; Michael Leibundgut, bass)

Herbei oh ihr Gläubigen (Adestes fideles)
For mixed chorus
1974
Duration: 3'30"

Anrufung I, II & III
For mixed chorus
1974, rev. 1995
Duration: 2', 2' and 3'30"

Hymnus (Venantius Fortunatus)
For mixed chorus
1979
Note: Also exists in a version from 1996 with solo tenor

Antiphon Joel II und Ruth Esther
For mixed chorus
1979, rev. 1988
Duration: 2'

Das Beinwurstlied (E. Hügli)
For men's chorus
1979, rev. 1991
Duration: 4'

Abschied vom Walde (Joseph von Eichendorff)
For mixed chorus
1984
Duration: 5'

Der Jäger Abschied (Joseph von Eichendorff)
1984
For mixed chorus
Duration: 4'

Spruch (Johann Wolfgang von Goethe)
For two-part men's or women's chorus
1987
Duration: 1'

Stadtbrunnen (Urs Martin Strub)
For men's chorus
1990
Duration: 2'

Lied der Flösser III (Urs Martin Strub)
For men's chorus
1991
Duration: 3'

Bap nos (Vater unser)
For mixed chorus
1992
Duration: 2'30"
For mixed chorus
Publ.: Musikverlag Müller & Schade M&S 1993
Recording: *Bap Nos. In memoriam Meinrad Schütter*, Guild Music GMCD 7349
(2010)

Adorazione dei pastori
For mixed chorus
1993
Duration: 3'
Note: Also exists in a version from 1996 with solo tenor
FP (version with solo tenor): 25 July 2008 in the Luisengymnasium, Munich. Tom
Amir (tenor); Chor Chantier Vocal, cond. Abélia Nordmann

Eines Strolches Trostlied (Walter Mehring)
For men's chorus
1993
Duration: 4'

Romanza. Itinéraire de Londres à Valparaiso, Fragment (Jean-Paul de Dadelsen)
For men's chorus
1994
Duration: 2'
FP: 1 April 2005 in the Gallery Maison 44, Basel (with four solo voices). Schubert
Quartet, Zurich (Frédéric Gindraux, Tino Brütsch, tenors; Samuel Zünd, baritone;
Michael Leibundgut, bass)

Auszug (Martin Schmid)
For mixed chorus
1998
Duration: 2'

Fürchte dich nicht (Martin Schmid)
For mixed chorus
1998

Zahme Xenien (Johann Wolfgang von Goethe)
For mixed chorus
1998
Duration: 1'

Publ.: Musikverlag Müller & Schade M&S 1470
FP: 18 December 1999 in the Zentralbibliothek Zürich. The Choir of Gonville and Caius College, Cambridge, cond. Geoffrey Webber

Zuspruch II (Nandor Währing)
For mixed chorus
1998
Duration: 3'30"

Das Ende des Festes (Conrad Ferdinand Meyer)
For men's chorus
2002
Duration: 2'
FP: 1 April 2005 in the Gallery Maison 44, Basel (with four solo voices). Schubert Quartet, Zurich (Frédéric Gindraux, Tino Brütsch, tenors; Samuel Zünd, baritone; Michael Leibundgut, bass)

Songs for Voice(s) and Ensemble or Orchestra
Serenade (Siegfried August Mahlmann)
For soprano, flute and viola
1934
Duration: 2'30"
FP: 28 July 1983 in Obersaxen at the International Summer Festival

Serenade (Hermann Hesse)
For voice and string trio (vn, va, vc)
1934, rev. 1970 and 2005
1. *Allegro moderato*
2. *Dreistimmige Musik*
3. *Allegro*
Duration: 11'
FP: 31 January 1986 in Chur. Helen Keller (soprano), Munich String Trio
Recording: *Bündner Komponisten*, Musikszene Schweiz/Ex Libris EL 16994 (LP; 1987)
Note: Only the second movement features the voice.

Vor der Ernte II (Martin Greif)
For soprano and string quartet or string orchestra
1936 (?)
Duration: 1'
FP: 5 May 1981 in Chur. Karin Ott (soprano), Camerata Zürich, cond. Räto Tschupp

Der Wunsch des Liebhabers (Hans Bethge, from the Chinese)
For soprano, flute, clarinet, viola, cello and piano; the viola and cello parts may be assigned to a larger body of players
1939
Duration: 2'

Dedication: 'To Mrs Barbara Wiesmann-Hunger'
FP: 5 May 1981 in Chur. Karin Ott (soprano), Camerata Zürich, cond. Räto Tschupp
Note: Also extant in a version for soprano and piano; > Songs for Voice and Piano

Sonett, 'Die Liebende schreibt' (Johann Wolfgang von Goethe)
For soprano and chamber orchestra
1939
Instr.: fl, ob, clar, bn – hn – str
Duration: 3'
FP: 5 May 1981 in Chur. Karin Ott (soprano), Camerata Zürich, cond. Räto Tschupp

Et incarnatus est (text from the Latin mass)
For solo soprano and chamber ensemble or chamber orchestra
1949
Instr.: fl, ob, vn 1, vn 2, va, vc, db (the string parts may be played by a string orchestra)
Duration: 6'
FP: 20 June 1949 at Radio Torino. Bettina Lupo (soprano), Silvio Clerici (flute), Giovanni Bongera (oboe), cond. Mario Salerno

Der Abend (René-Louis Piachaud, trans. Max Geilinger)
For baritone and orchestra
1971
Instr.: 2 fl, ob, 2 clar, bn – hn – perc – hp – str
Duration: 5'

Geburtstagslied (Johann Wolfgang von Goethe)
For soprano solo and strings
1975
Duration: 4'
Dedication: 'To my friend Philipp Zinsli'
FP: 5 May 1981 in Chur. Karin Ott (soprano), Camerata Zürich, cond. Räto Tschupp

Fuge (Johann Wolfgang von Goethe)
For soprano, bass, speaker and string trio
1976
Dedication: 'To my dear friend Philipp Zinsli on his 61st birthday'

Laudatio (Meinrad Schütter)
For voice (or speaker), violin, viola and cello
1976
Dedication: 'To the Barandun family and the Stradivarius Trio'

Kriminal-Gedichte (M. E. Bachmann)
For speaker and chamber ensemble

1983
Instr.: fl, ob, hn, tpt, timp, perc, vn, vc, pf

Scenic Cantata (the *Medicinal Cantata*) (Meinrad Schütter)
For voice, speaker, flute, piano and harpsichord (also with the option of adding 'two to three strings and percussion as desired')
1985
Duration: 15'30"
FP: 22 March 1985 in Chur

Pastorale IV. Adorazione dei pastori II (Laudario di Cortona)
For voice and strings
1988
Duration: 3'
Dedication: 'To Father Karl Weber'

Quiete (Giuseppe Ungaretti)
For voice, flute, violin, viola and cello (or flute and string orchestra)
1991
Duration: 2'
Dedication: 'To my dear wife Claudia'
Recording: *Meinrad Schütter: Kammermusik und instrumental begleitete Gesänge 1939–1998*, Swisspan 510 316 (2000)

Der Steinsammler (Nelly Sachs)
For contralto or mezzosoprano, tenor, flute and piano
1997
Duration: 6'
FP: 22 April 1997 in Kyiv (Ukraine). Ana-Salina Sabati (contralto), Otto Georg Linsi (tenor), Carsten Hustedt (flute) and Martin-Lucas Staub (piano)
Recording: *Meinrad Schütter: Kammermusik und instrumental begleitete Gesänge 1939–1998*, Swisspan 510 316 (2000)

Gedenk (Joseph von Eichendorff)
For low voice, horn and piano or organ
2001
Publ.: Musikverlag Müller & Schade M&S 2353

Gesang (Hermann Kükelhaus)
For voice, cello and piano
2001
Duration: 4'
FP: 1 September 2002 at 'Art Rü' in Rünenberg (Canton Baselland). Stefania Huonder (mezzo-soprano), Jarmo Vainio (cello), Ute Stoecklin (piano)

Fern im Osten wird es helle (Novalis)
For voice, flute and piano
2001

Duration: 3'
Publ. Musikverlag Müller & Schade M&S 2381
Dedication: 'For Ute and Susanne Stoecklin'
FP: 21 December 2003 at the Gallery Maison 44 in Basel. Stefania Huonder (mezzosoprano), Miriam Terragni (flute), Ute Stoecklin (piano)

Works for Speaker with Accompaniment
Porcorum causa (Albert Vigoleis Thelen)
For speaker and piano
1983

Aus den Weihnachtsbriefen an Frieda Mermet (Robert Walser)
For speaker, flute and piano
1998
Duration: 4'
Publ.: Musikverlag Nepomuk MN 12033
Dedication: 'To Ute Stoecklin'
FP: 24 January 1999 in Basel. Carsten Hustedt (flute), Ute Stoecklin (piano)
Note: A version exists for speaker, flute, string quartet and piano that the composer later declared 'invalid'

Am Gürtel Orions (Andreas Neeser)
For cello and speaker or 'speaking cellist'
2004
Duration: 5'
Publ.: Musikverlag Nepomuk MN 12059
FP: 19 December 2004 in the Gallery Maison 44, Basel. Christiane Moreno (speaker), Martin Merker (cello)
Recording: with Andreas Neeser and Martin Merker, *Grenzland – Ein Klangbuch*, Neue Impulse Verlag, Essen, 2007

Grundungen (Andreas Neeser)
For cello and speaker
2005
Duration: 7'
Publ.: Musikverlag Nepomuk MN 12060
FP: 8 November 2005 in the Gemeindebibliothek in Wettingen. Andreas Neeser (speaker), Martin Merker (cello)
Recording: with Andreas Neeser and Martin Merker, *Grenzland – Ein Klangbuch*, Neue Impulse Verlag, Essen, 2007

Songs for Voice and Organ
Where no voice type is indicated below, the composer has specified none for the work in question.

Ave Maria (anon., fifteenth century)
For soprano and organ or piano

1939, rev. 1968
Dedication: To Constanta Brancovici
Duration: 2'

Choral I & II: Mit meinem Gott
For voice and organ or piano
1940
Duration: 3'

Triptychon
For soprano (only the second movement) and organ
1952
1. *Praeludium*
FP: 1975 in Chur. Gion Antoni Derungs (organ)
2. *Wanderers Nachtlied* (Johann Wolfgang von Goethe)
FP: 20 September 1953 in Chur. Claudia Schütter-Mengelt (soprano), Lucius Juon
(organ)
3. *Postludium*
FP: 1958 in Zurich. Martin Ruhoff (organ)
Duration (complete): 7'30"
Note: The second movement is an arrangement of Schütter's setting for men's
chorus and orchestra of 1948

Psalm. The Annunciation of Maria
For mezzo-soprano and organ
1958, rev. 1994
Duration: 1'30"

Le Chapelet (trad., Brittany)
For soprano and organ
1971
Duration: 2'
Dedication: 'To Pfarrer Emil Huber (Don Emilio)'

Erhebung (Urs Martin Strub)
For medium voice and organ
1977, rev. 1994
Duration: 1'30"
Dedication: 'In memoriam Rudolf Jakob Humm'

Abendlied (Urs Martin Strub)
For medium voice and organ
1983
Duration: 1'50"

Herbei, oh ihr Gläubigen. Adeste fideles
1985
Duration: 3'

Dedication: 'To Dr Willy Keller'

Gedenk (Joseph von Eichendorff)
For low voice, horn and organ (or piano)
2001
Duration: 2'
Publ.: Musikverlag Müller & Schade M&S 2352

Songs for Voice and Piano
Where no voice type is indicated below, the composer has specified none for the
work in question.

Dumonda (Gian Caduff)
For high voice and piano
1931
Duration: 2'30"
Dedication: 'To Claudia Mengelt'
Publ: Musikedition Nepomuk, in *Ausgewählte Lieder*, Vol. 1, No. 5, MN 9260
Recordings: *Meinrad Schütter: Lieder*, Uranus 602 (1997); *Hesperos: 20th-Century
Songs – Switzerland*, Guild Music GMCD 7254 (2003); and *Duo en treis – Duo zu
dritt*, Swisspan 51 723 (2006)

Als er seiner Magdalis nichts zum grünen Donnerstag schenken konnte (Johann
Christian Günther)
For medium voice and piano
1933
Publ: Musikedition Nepomuk, in *Ausgewählte Lieder*, Vol. 3, No. 4, MN 9723

Hochzeitslied (from the Yugoslavian)
For high or medium voice and piano
1933, rev. 1935
Duration: 2'
Publ: Musikedition Nepomuk, in *Ausgewählte Lieder*, Vol. 3, No. 1, MN 9723

Minnelied (anon.)
1933, rev. 1970
Duration: 1'30"

Abgrund (Nandor Währing)
For medium voice and piano
1934/1939
Publ: Musikedition Nepomuk, in *Ausgewählte Lieder*, Vol. 2, No. 4, MN 9261
Recording: *Meinrad Schütter: Lieder*, Uranus 602 (1997)

Die müden Sterne (Karl Stamm)
1934
Duration: 2'
Publ: Musikedition Nepomuk, in *Ausgewählte Lieder*, Vol. 2, No. 2, MN 9261

Ernste Stunde (Rainer Maria Rilke)
For medium voice and piano
1934
Duration: 2'
Publ: Musikedition Nepomuk, in *Ausgewählte Lieder*, Vol. 1, No. 3, MN 9260
Recordings: *Meinrad Schütter: Lieder*, Uranus 602 (1997), and *Duo en treis – Duo zu dritt*, Swisspan 51 723 (2006)

Herbsttag (Rainer Maria Rilke)
For medium voice and piano
1934
Duration: 2'
Publ: Musikedition Nepomuk, in *Ausgewählte Lieder*, Vol. 1, No. 2, MN 9260
Recordings: *Meinrad Schütter: Lieder*, Uranus 602 (1997); *Hesperos: 20th-Century Songs – Switzerland*, Guild Music GMCD 7254 (2003); and *Duo en treis – Duo zu dritt*, Swisspan 51 723 (2006)

Morgentau (Karl Stamm)
For medium voice and piano
1934
Duration: 2'
Publ: Musikedition Nepomuk, in *Ausgewählte Lieder*, Vol. 2, No. 1, MN 9261
Recordings: *Meinrad Schütter: Lieder*, Uranus 602, and *Duo en treis – Duo zu dritt*, Swisspan 51 723

Südliches Glockenspiel (Karl Stamm)
For medium voice and piano
1934
Duration: 2'30"
Publ: Musikedition Nepomuk, in *Ausgewählte Lieder*, Vol. 2, No. 3, MN 9261
Recordings: *Meinrad Schütter: Lieder*, Uranus 602, and *Duo en treis – Duo zu dritt*, Swisspan 51 723

Vorfrühling (Max Dauthendey)
For medium voice and piano
1934
Duration: 2'30"
Dedication: 'To Barbara Wiesmann-Hunger'
Publ: Musikedition Nepomuk, in *Ausgewählte Lieder*, Vol. 1, No. 1, MN 9260
Recordings: *Meinrad Schütter: Lieder*, Uranus 602 (1997), and *Duo en treis – Duo zu dritt*, Swisspan 51 723 (2006)
Note: Also exists in a version of 1934 for high voice.

Vier alte Spielmannsweisen
1. Wess' Leben so sich endet (Wolfram von Eschenbach), 1934/1970
2. Deutsche Spielmannsweise No. 1. Chançona tedesca (Walther von der Vogelweide), 1934

3. Deutsche Spielmannsweise No. 2. (Neidhart von Reuental), 1995
4. Minnelied (anon.), 1933/1970
For medium voice and piano
Duration: 4'30"
Recording (only No. 4): *Meinrad Schütter: Lieder*, Uranus 602 (1997)

Vor der Ernte (Martin Greif)
For high or medium voice and piano
1936
Duration: 1'
Publ: Musikedition Nepomuk, in *Ausgewählte Lieder*, Vol. 3, No. 2, MN 9723
Recording: *Meinrad Schütter: Lieder*, Uranus 602 (1997)

Kyrie (Martin Schmid)
For high or medium voice and piano
1938
Duration: 2'
Publ: Musikedition Nepomuk, in *Ausgewählte Lieder*, Vol. 3, No. 3, MN 9723

Der Wunsch des Liebhabers (Hans Bethge, from the Chinese)
For high or medium voice and piano
1939
Duration: 2'
Dedication: 'To Mrs Barbara Wiesmann-Hunger'
Note: Also extant in an arrangement for soprano and ensemble > Songs for Voice
and Ensemble or Orchestra

Lamentatiun dal pulin, dall'ochetta e dal pulaster (trad. Rumansh)
For high or medium voice and piano
1943/1944
Duration: 3'
Dedication: 'To Mr Hans Weber'
Publ: Musikedition Nepomuk, in *Ausgewählte Lieder*, Vol. 6, No. 3, MN 12066

Zwei Bündner Scherzlieder
1. Es wird si ätte muusä (folksong)
2. Das Langwieser Lied (folksong)
1944
Duration: 5'
Publ: Musikedition Nepomuk, in *Ausgewählte Lieder*, Vol. 6, Nos. 1 and 2, MN
12066

Fragment I (Nandor Währing)
For baritone and piano
1955, rev. 1957
Duration: 1'

Matg (Gian Caduff)
For high voice and piano
1955, rev. 1977
Duration: 3'
Note: Schütter has here adapted a melody by Wilhelm Weismann
Recordings: *Meinrad Schütter: Lieder*, Uranus 602 and *Duo en treis – Duo zu dritt*,
Swisspan 51 723

Der Tod (Matthias Claudius)
For medium voice and piano
1956, rev. 1976
Duration: 1'30"
Publ: Musikedition Nepomuk, in *Ausgewählte Lieder*, Vol. 1, No. 4, MN 9260
Recordings: *Meinrad Schütter: Lieder*, Uranus 602 (1997); *Hesperos: 20th-Century
Songs – Switzerland*, Guild Music GMCD 7254 (2003); and *Duo en treis – Duo zu
dritt*, Swisspan 51 723 (2006)

Sehnsucht (Gebhard Karst)
For high or medium voice and piano
1960, rev. 1996
Duration: 2'
Publ: Musikedition Nepomuk, in *Ausgewählte Lieder*, Vol. 4, No. 3, MN 9724
Recording: *Meinrad Schütter: Lieder*, Uranus 602 (1997)

Pos o matg (Gian Caduff)
For medium voice and piano
1962
Duration: 3'30"
Recordings: *Meinrad Schütter: Lieder*, Uranus 602 (1997), and *Duo en
treis – Duo zu dritt*, Swisspan 51 723 (2006)

Hat Münchhausen wirklich gelogen (Max Mumenthaler)
Ballad for baritone and piano
1965, rev. 1974
Duration: 7'
Dedication: 'To Eduard Spörri'

Zwei Stern lüchtend hoch am Himmel (trad.)
For voice and piano
1965
Dedication: 'To Martin Schmid'

Brotspruch (Max Mumenthaler)
For high voice and piano
1970
Duration: 2'

Sonett (Pierre Walter Müller)
For soprano and piano

1970
Duration: 3'

Da geht der Zug der Brüder (Martin Schmid)
For soprano and piano
1979
Duration: 3'

Denn: Aller Anfang ist schwer (Walter Mehring)
For medium voice and piano
1980, rev. 1989
Duration: 3'
Publ: Musikedition Nepomuk, Aarau, in *Ausgewählte Lieder*, Vol. 2, No. 5, MN 9261
Recording: *Meinrad Schütter: Lieder*, Uranus 602 (1997)

Nächtliche Lampe (Albert Vigoleis Thelen)
For high or medium voice and piano
1980
Duration: 3'
Publ: Musikedition Nepomuk, in *Ausgewählte Lieder*, Vol. 5, No. 4, MN 9725
Recordings: *Meinrad Schütter: Lieder*, Uranus 602 (1997), and *Hesperos: 20th-Century Songs – Switzerland*, Guild Music GMCD 7254 (2003)

Chanson (Max Mumenthaler)
1981
Duration: 3'30"
Publ: Musikedition Nepomuk, in *Ausgewählte Lieder*, Vol. 5, No. 2, MN 9725
Recording: *Meinrad Schütter: Lieder*, Uranus 602 (1997)

Lied der Flösser (Urs Martin Strub)
For high voice and piano
1981
Duration: 2'
Publ: Musikedition Nepomuk, in *Ausgewählte Lieder*, Vol. 6 No. 5, MN 12066

Plainte et complainte d'un pauv' vieux chien (Walter Mehring)
For high or medium voice and piano
1985 rev. 1996
Duration: 2'
Publ: Musikedition Nepomuk, in *Ausgewählte Lieder*, Vol. 5 No. 3, MN 9725
Recording: *Meinrad Schütter: Lieder*, Uranus 602 (1997)

In der Hängematte (Richard Münch)
For medium voice and piano
1989
Duration: 2'30"
Publ: Musikedition Nepomuk, in *Ausgewählte Lieder*, Vol. 2, No. 6, MN 9261

Recordings: *Meinrad Schütter: Lieder*, Uranus 602 (1997), and *Duo en treis – Duo zu dritt*, Swisspan 51 723 (2006)

Phoenix (Flandrina von Salis)
Five songs for mezzo-soprano and piano
1. Ich trage deinen Namen
2. Sommer (In die Wolken)
3. Beuge dein Antlitz
4. Lass mich Gitarre sein
5. Nichts
1991
Duration: 11'
FP: 26 October 1991 in Malans. Stefania Huonder (mezzo), Beatrice Kurth (piano)
Publ: Musikedition Nepomuk MN 12067

Reisen (Robert Walser)
For high or medium voice and piano
1991
Duration: 2'30"
Dedication: 'To Dr Fritz Hermann-Ambühl'
Publ: Musikedition Nepomuk, in *Ausgewählte Lieder*, Vol. 5, No. 1, MN 9725
Recording: *Meinrad Schütter: Lieder*, Uranus 602 (1997)

Herbst-Haiku (Flandrina von Salis)
For medium or high voice and piano
1993
Duration: 2'30"
Publ: Musikedition Nepomuk, in *Ausgewählte Lieder*, Vol. 4, No. 1, MN 9724

Urworte Orphisch (Johann Wolfgang von Goethe)
For medium voice and piano
1993
Duration: 3'
Dedication: 'For Ruth Barandun'

Ein Blick (Eric Waldmann)
For high or medium voice and piano
1994
Duration: 2'
Note: first version.

Chanzuns da la not (Andri Peer)
Three songs in Rumansh
1. L'Alba
2. Zona dal plaschair
3. Favuogn
1994
Duration: 11'

FP: 20 September 1995 in the Konzertstudio in Chur. Stefania Huonder (mezzo), Ute Stoecklin (piano)
Dedication: 'For Stefania Huonder and Ute Stoecklin'
Publ: Musikedition Nepomuk MN 9602
Recordings: (Nos. 1–3) *Meinrad Schütter: Lieder*, Uranus 602 (1997); *Duo en treis – Duo zu dritt*, Swisspan 51 723 (2006); *Meinrad Schütter: Kammermusik und instrumental begleitete Gesänge*, Swisspan 510 316 (2000); (Nos. 2 and 3 only) *Hesperos: 20th-Century Songs – Switzerland*, Guild Music GMCD 7254 (2003)

Ein Blick (Eric Waldmann)
For tenor and piano
1996
Duration: 2′
Note: second version.
Publ: Musikedition Nepomuk, in *Ausgewählte Lieder*, Vol. 4, No. 2, MN 9724
Recording: *Meinrad Schütter: Lieder*, Uranus 602 (1997)

Schmetterling (Nelly Sachs)
For mezzo-soprano and piano
1997
Duration: 3′
FP: 27 September 1997 in Ratzeburg, Schleswig-Holstein. Stefania Huonder (mezzo-soprano), Ute Stoecklin (piano)
Recording: *Meinrad Schütter: Kammermusik und instrumental begleitete Gesänge 1939–1998*, Swisspan 510 316 (2000)

Nämlich (Hans Magnus Enzensberger)
For bass and piano
1998, rev. 2002

Discography

In 2019, the Swiss radio stations from all four language regions of the country launched a web-based platform, 'neo.mx3' (at https://neo.mx3.ch/), to make accessible radio recordings of Swiss music that are held in their archives. At the time of publication, numerous works by Schütter had been uploaded onto this platform (at https://neo.mx3.ch/meisch), though most of them had previously been released on CD (all these CDs are listed below). Some recordings, however, were made for broadcast purposes only and were never commercially released. These are listed in the Work Catalogue above in the entry for the individual works in question.

Bündner Komponisten
Includes Schütter's *Serenade for Voice and String Trio*
Helen Keller (soprano), Munich String Trio (Ana Chumachenko, violin; Oscar Lysi, viola; Wolfgang Mehlhorn, cello)
LP
Zurich: Ex Libris EL 16994 (1987)

Meinrad Schütter: Lieder
CD
Features the following songs by Schütter:
Dumonda, Hochzeitslied, Südliches Glockenspiel, Morgentau, Vorfrühling, Herbsttag, Ernste Stunde, Abgrund, Minnelied, Vor der Ernte, Kyrie, Matg, Pos, o matg, Nächtliche Lampe, Der Tod, Denn: Aller Anfang ist schwer, Plainte et complainte, Chanson, Reisen, Sehnsucht, Ein Blick, In der Hängematte, Chanzuns da la not (L'alba, Zona dal plaschair, Favuogn).
Karin Ott (soprano), Stefania Huonder (mezzo-soprano), Otto Georg Linsi (tenor), Ute Stoecklin (piano), Janka Wyttenbach (piano)
Zurich: Uranus 602 (1997)

Christ Ascended: Swiss Religious Music of the 20th Century
CD
Includes Schütter's organ pieces *Partita 'Mit meinem Gott geh ich zur Ruh'* and *Adorazione dei pastori*.
Timothy Uglow, organ.
St. Helier, Jersey: Guild Music GMCG 7177 (1999)

Meinrad Schütter: Kammermusik und instrumental begleitete Gesänge 1939–1998
CD
Contents: Suite No. 1 for Clarinet and Piano; Duo for Flute and Cello; *Clavis astartis magica II* for Solo Violin; *Quiete* for Voice, Flute and String Trio; *Chanzuns da la not* (*L'alba, Zona dal plaschair, Favuogn*) for mezzo-soprano and piano; Two Songs to Texts by Nelly Sachs (*Schmetterling* and *Der Steinsammler*); *Poema* for Flute and Piano; Piano Trio; Trio for Three Clarinets.
Stefania Huonder (mezzo-soprano), Niklaus Rüegg (tenor), Michael Leibundgut (bass), Carsten Hustedt (flute), Hans Rudolf Stalder (clarinet), Mathias Müller (clarinet), Elmar Schmid (clarinet), Ada Pesch (violin, viola), Dorota Sosnowska (violin), Martin Merker (cello), Jarmo Vainio (cello), Martin Derungs (piano), Ute Stoecklin (piano), Helena Maffli-Nissinen (piano), Fennica Trio
Zurich: Swisspan 510 316 (2000)

Schütter, Schaeuble: Klavierkonzerte
CD
Includes Schütter's Piano Concerto and his *Pastorale II* for solo clarinet and string orchestra.
Antoine Rebstein (piano), Josias Just (clarinet), Zurich Chamber Orchestra, cond. Howard Griffiths
Zurich: Musikszene Schweiz/Migros-Genossenschafts-Bund MGB CD 6162 (2000)

Hesperos: 20th-Century Songs – Switzerland
CD
Includes the following songs by Schütter: *Dumonda, Herbsttag, Der Tod, Die müden Sterne, Nächtliche Lampe, Zona dal plaschair, Favuogn*
Michael Leibundgut (bass), Ute Stoecklin (piano)
Ramsen: Guild Music GMCD 7254 (2003)

Duo en treis – Duo zu dritt
CD
Includes the following songs by Schütter: *Vorfrühling, In der Hängematte, Herbst-Haiku, Herbsttag, Pos o Matg, Matg, Morgentau, Die müden Sterne, Südliches Glockenspiel, Dumonda, Chanzuns da la not* (*L'alba, Zona dal plaschair, Favuogn*), *Ernste Stunde, Der Tod*
Neuhausen: Quantaphon/Swisspan 51 723 (2006)

20th century Swiss String Quartets
CD
Includes Schütter's String Quartet
Casal Quartet
Ramsen: Guild Music GMCD 7254 (2006)

Grenzland – Ein Klangbuch
CD
Includes Schütter's *Am Gürtel Orions* and *Grundungen*
Andreas Neeser (speaker), Martin Merker (cello)
Zurich: Wolfbach-Verlag (2007)

Bap Nos. In memoriam Meinrad Schütter
CD
Includes Schütter's *Bap Nos (Vater unser)* and his *Grosse Messe*
Cappella Nova, cond. Raphael Immoos, Susanne Doll (organ)
Ramsen: Guild Music GMCD 7349 (2010)

Spiritoso!
CD
Includes Mozart's Flute Concerto, K313, with three cadenzas by Schütter, also published as *Promenades à Mannheim avec Mozart*, and Carl Stamitz's Flute Concerto Op. 29 with three cadenzas by Schütter, also published as *Promenades à Mannheim avec Stamitz*
Carsten Hustedt (flute), St Christopher Chamber Orchestra, Vilnius, cond. Donatus Katkus
Mannheim: RBM Musikproduktion CD RBM 463042/43 (double album; 2012)

Select
Bibliography

ADORNO, THEODOR W., ed. Richard Leppert, *Essays on Music*, University of California Press, Berkeley, 2002

BROTBECK, ROMAN, *Töne und Schälle. Robert Walser-Vertonungen 1912 bis 2021*, Brill Fink, Paderborn, 2021

BRUNNER, LINUS, and TOTH, ALFRED, *Die rätische Sprache – enträtselt*, Amt für Kulturpflege des Kantons St Gallen, St Gallen, 1987

EIDENBENZ, MICHAEL, 'Freiheit und Glück einer eigenen Sprache. Der Komponist Meinrad Schütter', *dissonanz*, No. 81 (June 2003), pp. 20–26

——, 'Ehrenrettung für eine vergessene Oper', *dissonanz*, No. 93 (March 2006), pp. 31–32

GARTMANN, THOMAS, 'Den Klangeigenschaften eines Akkords nachspüren', in *Moi! Kulturmagazin Graubünden*, No. 5 (1990)

——, 'Freisetzung linearer Dimensionen. Zum 80. Geburtstag des Komponisten Meinrad Schütter', in *Neue Zürcher Zeitung*, Vol. 211, No. 219 (21 September 1990)

KRAMREITER, TOMÁS, 'Erinnerung an Meinrad Schütter', in Ute Stoecklin, *Meinrad Schütter 1910–2006*, p. 174

MESSIAEN, OLIVIER, trans. SATTERFIELD, JOHN, *The Technique of my Musical Language*, Vol. 1. Alphonse Leduc, Paris, 1956

PALAZZETTI, NICOLÒ, *Béla Bartók in Italy: The Politics of Myth-Making*, The Boydell Press, Woodbridge, 2021

PALMER, PETER, Untitled review of assorted CDs of Swiss music in *Tempo*, No. 218 (October 2001), pp. 56–58

——, untitled review of three CDs of Swiss music in *Tempo*, No. 238 (October 2006), pp. 48–49

PEER, OSCAR, 'Erinnerungen an den Schützenweg 15 in Chur', in *Bündner Jahrbuch: Zeitschrift für Kunst, Kultur und Geschichte* No. 53 (2011), p. 166

RUBELI, ALFRED. *Paul Hindemith und Zürich*, Hug, Zurich, 1969

RUHOFF, MARTIN ('mr'), 'Kammerchor Chur', in *Neue Zürcher Zeitung*, Vol. 196, No. 280 (2 December 1975)

——, 'Uraufführung einer Messe', in *Neue Zürcher Zeitung*, Vol. 202, No. 22, (28 January 1981)

SCHACHER, THOMAS, 'Klingendes Waldsterben', in *Neue Zürcher Zeitung*, Vol. 221, No. 243 (18 October 2000)

SCHRÖDER, LOTHAR: *Vigoleis – ein Wiedergänger Don Quijotes: Eine Untersuchung zum literarischen Lebensweg des Helden im Prosawerk Albert Vigoleis Thelens*, Grupello Verlag, Düsseldorf, 2007

SCHUH, WILLI, 'Neue Schweizer Musik' in *Neue Zürcher Zeitung*, Vol. 160, No. 587, 'Second Sunday edition' (2 April 1939)

STOECKLIN, UTE, *Meinrad Schütter 1910–2006. Lebenswerk Musik oder 'Die Kunst, sich nicht stören zu lassen'*, Musikverlag Müller & Schade, Bern, 2010

VERAGUTH, MANFRED, '"Ich werde dieses Bündnerparadies wohl zu behandeln Wissen": der Nachlass Meinrad Schütter (1910–2006) im Stadtarchiv Chur', in *Bündner Monatsblatt: Zeitschrift für Bündner Geschichte, Landeskunde und Baukultur* No. 3 (2016), pp. 343–51

WILLIMANN, JOSEPH, *Pro Musica. Der neuen Musik zulieb. 50 Jahre Pro Musica. Ortsgruppe Zürich der Internationalen Gesellschaft für Neue Musik (IGNM)*, Atlantis Musikbuch-Verlag, Zurich, 1988

ZIMMERLIN, ALFRED, 'Ein Einzelgänger. Zum Tod des Komponisten Meinrad Schütters', in *Neue Zürcher Zeitung*, Vol. 227, No. 11 (14–15 January 2006)

ZINSLI, PHILIPP, *Meinrad Schütter: Freund Meini Schütter zum 80. Wiegenfest mit herzlichen Wünschen zugeeignet vom Zinsli-Clan*, Selbstverlag, Chur, 1990

ZSCHOKKE, HEINRICH, *Eine Selbstschau*, Sauerländer, Aarau, 1842

ZÜLLIG, WALTER, 'Philosophische Klänge von Hindemith und Schütter', *Bündner-Zeitung* (18 September 1990)

Index
of Schütter's Works

Operas

Flüchtlinge, Die, 73, 75, 97, 138
Medea, 54, 59–61, 63, 66, 72, 73, 94,
  126–28, 130, 132, 137
Rübezahl, 138

Ballets

Clownesque, 139
Dr Joggeli sött go Birli schüttle, 72, 73, 138

Orchestral Works

Concentus, 99, 102, 140
Fuge > Ricercare No. 1
Fünf Varianten und Metamorphose, 43, 52,
  53, 102, 139
March No. 1, 139
March No. 2, 140
Metamorphosis, 99, 102, 140
Pastorale I. Adorazione dei pastori II, 140
Pastorale III. Adorazione dei pastori IV,
  102, 140
Ricercare No. 1, 53, 139
Suite for Small Orchestra, 79, 139
Symphony in One Movement, 108, 119,
  121, 122, 134, 139

Concertos

Duo Concertante 'Quasi una Fantasia', 79,
  96, 140
Pastorale II. Adorazione dei pastori III for
  clarinet and string orchestra, 102, 141,
  170
Piano Concerto, 24, 75, 96–101, 103, 108,
  133, 134, 140, 170

**Chamber Music and Works
for Solo Strings or Winds**

Antiquarisch for two clarinets and
  bassoon, 143
Bagatelle for horn and piano, 108, 145
Clavis Astartis magica I for violin and
  piano, 142
Clavis Astartis magica II for violin solo,
  142, 170
Consolazione for clarinet and organ, 112,
  145
Duo for Flute and Cello, after a scene in
  Aristophanes' Frogs, 116, 146, 170
Fanfares for brass and timpani, 92, 125,
  147
First Suite for clarinet and piano, 58, 141,
  170
Four Pieces for Clarinet, 95, 133, 134, 143
*Gommer Suite (Dix miniatures
  valaisannes)* for flute, violin and viola,
  118, 146
Herbei, oh ihr Gläubigen, for clarinet and
  organ, 145
Herbei, oh ihr Gläubigen, for violin,
  clarinet and organ, 142
Humoreske (Hommage à Francis Poulenc)
  for clarinet and piano, 102, 144
Invention I for two clarinets in B flat, 142
Invention II for oboe and two clarinets in
  B flat, 142
Invention III for flute and piano, 144
Invention IV for clarinet and piano, 145
Kanon (Spruch) for violin and clarinet,
  143
Kinderlied for trumpet and piano,, 145
Metamorphosis II for string quartet, 102,
  144
Nachtstücke I und II (Spiegelungen) for
  flute, clarinet and piano/harpsichord,
  102, 143
Notturno for violin and piano, 144
Phantasie for oboe d'amore and piano, 141
Piece for cello and piano, 146
Poema for flute and piano, 145, 170
Promenades à Mannheim for solo flute,
  118, 146, 171
Quartet for oboe, trumpet, bassoon and
  cello, 86, 125, 126, 147
Ricercare No. 2 for oboe, clarinet, horn
  and bassoon, 95, 142
Romance for horn and piano, 108, 145

Second Suite for clarinet and piano, 95, 143

Separate Einbildungen for clarinet, violin, cello and piano, 122, 146

Serenade for flute, oboe and clarinet, 95, 141

Sonata for Cello and Piano, 102, 143

String Quartet, 103, 134, 144, 170

Suite for cello solo, 142

Suite for solo flute, 147

Trio for three clarinets (or basset horns), 88, 108, 144, 170

Trio in One Movement for violin, cello and piano, 109, 135, 145, 170

Two Pieces for cello and piano, 141

Verbunkos (Chanson et danse hongroise) for violin and piano, 141

Widmung for two violins and viola, 142

Wind Octet, 95, 96, 143

Organ Works

Adorazione dei Pastori, 147, 169

Antienne du chant grigorien, 147

De Leonardo Pisano, 125, 148

Meditation, 125, 148

Novellette, 148

Partita, 'Mit meinem Gott geh' ich zur Ruh', 147

Postludium, 148

Piano Duets and Duos

Foxtrott, collage d'après 'Les enfants et les Sortilèges' de M. Ravel et un noël, 148

Introduzione e Passacaglia from the ballet *Dr Joggeli sött go Birli schüttle*, 148

Verbunkos for piano duet, 39, 148

Piano Solo

Albumblatt, 150

Anagramm, 151

Auf ein altes Bild, 103, 151

Bernadetten-Lieder, 151

Canto ermetico, 151

Churer Legende von Spukgeistern und Spiegeleien, 90, 150

Five Little Variations on a Children's Song, 150

Five Persian Songs and Dances, 150

Four Piano Pieces, 103, 151

Four Small Pieces, 148

Fugue, 150

Hommage à Paul Hindemith, 148

Jul-Lied für Kaya, 151

Kinderreigen im Hinterhof, 148

Monsieur Fibonacci fait ses compliments pour le cinquième anniversaire de Mlle Kaya, 151

Musik für Klavier in einer 'Nicht-nicht-Form', 150

Nachmittag eines Clavizimbels, 150

'... oder wie die Zeit vergeht', 103, 151

Passacaglia, 149

Petite scène alpestre, 149

Portugiesische Weihnacht, 151

Praeludium, 150

Präludium und Postludium, 149

Raumspielmusik, 150

Regentag im Schrebergarten, 149

Ricercare No. 3, 151

Six Variations on the Portuguese Christmas Carol 'Adeste fideles', 149

Sonata, 49, 149

Sonatina, 55, 132, 149

Study, 103, 151

Tanz der Spukgeister im Scaläratobel, 103, 151

Tanzstück, 150

Variations on a Rhythm, 96, 103, 150

Choral Works with Accompaniment

5 Variations on 'Macht hoch die Tür', 153

Adorazione dei pastori, 153

Chor seliger Knaben heiliger Anachoreten (Pater Seraphicus), 153

Da geht der Zug der Brüder, 152

Grosse Messe, 54, 55, 94, 122, 152, 171

Herbei, oh ihr Gläubigen (Adeste Fideles), 152

Kleine Messe, 153

Liebe leidet nicht, Gesellen, 152

Lied der Flösser II, 152

Lied der Flösser IV, 153

Morgen, 16n, 153

Neujahr, 152

Pascas, 153

Porcorum causa, 87, 152

Wanderers Nachtlied, 66, 152

Choral Works *a cappella*

Abschied vom Walde, 155

Ach Mutter, gib mir keinen Mann, 154

Adorazione dei pastori, 156

Anrufung I, II & III, 155

Antiphon Joel II und Ruth Esther, 155

Auszug, 156

Bap nos (Vater unser), 156, 171

Beinwurstlied, Das, 155

Choral I, 'Mit meinem Gott geh ich zur

Ruh', 153, 169
*Choral II, 'Ach komm füll unsere Seelen
    ganz'*, 66, 153
Ende des Festes, Das, 157
Fürchte dich nicht, 156
Herbei oh ihr Gläubigen (Adestes fideles),
    155
Hymnus, 155
Hymnus 'Tantum ergo', 72, 154
Jäger Abschied, Der, 155
Lied der Flösser III, 156
Offertorium 'Ad ducam eos', 154
Ögls e stailas, 72, 154
*Romanza. Itinéraire de Londres à
    Valparaiso, Fragment*, 156
Schwere Nacht, 154
Spruch, 155
Stadtbrunnen, 155
Strolches Trostlied, Eines, 85, 156
Trost, 154
Zahme Xenien, 156
Zuspruch, 72, 154, 157
Zuspruch II, 39
Zwischen Berg und tiefem Tal, 154

**Songs for Voice(s) and Ensemble
or Orchestra**
Et incarnatus est, 66, 158
Fern im Osten wird es helle, 159
Fuge, 158
Geburtstagslied, 158
Gedenk, 159
Gesang, 159
Kriminal-Gedichte, 158
Laudatio, 158
Pastorale IV. Adorazione dei pastori II, 159
*Prostate Cantata > Scenic Cantata
    (Medicinal Cantata)*
Quiete, 159, 170
Scenic Cantata (Medicinal Cantata), 95,
    96, 159
Serenade for soprano, flute and viola, 157
Serenade for voice and string trio, 49, 91,
    126, 130, 131, 157, 169
Sonett, 'Die Liebende schreibt', 55, 158
Steinsammler, Der, 114, 159, 170
Vor der Ernte II, 157
Wunsch des Liebhabers, Der, 157

Works for Speaker with Accompaniment
Am Gürtel Orions, 125, 160, 170
*Aus den Weihnachtsbriefen an Frieda
    Mermet*, 117, 160
Grundungen, 125, 160, 170

Porcorum causa, 160

Songs for Voice and Organ
Abendlied, 161
Ave Maria, 55, 160
Chapelet, Le, 161
Choral I & II, Mit meinem Gott, 161
Erhebung, 161
Gedenk, 162
Herbei, oh ihr Gläubigen. Adeste fideles,
    162
Psalm. The Annunciation of Maria, 161
Triptychon, 72, 161
Wanderers Nachtlied, 72, 161

Songs for Voice and Piano
Abgrund, 39, 162, 169
Alba, L', 111, 167, 169, 170
*Als er seiner Magdalis nichts zum Grünen
    Donnerstag schenken konnte*, 45, 162
Beuge dein Antlitz, 167
Blick, Ein, 167–69
Brotspruch, 165
Chanson, 166, 169
Chanzuns da la not, 61, 93, 110, 111, 131,
    167, 169, 170
Da geht der Zug der Brüder, 166
Denn: Aller Anfang ist schwer, 84, 166, 169
*Deutsche Spielmannsweise No. 1:
    Chançona tedesca*, 163
Deutsche Spielmannsweise No. 2, 164
Dumonda, 45–48, 110, 130, 162, 169, 170
Ernste Stunde, 48, 163, 169, 170
Es wird si ätte muusä, 66, 164
Favuogn, 112, 167, 169, 170
Fragment I, 40, 164
Hat Münchhausen wirklich gelogen, 165
Herbst-Haiku, 167, 170
Herbsttag, 45, 163, 169, 170
Hochzeitslied (from the Yugoslavian), 38,
    45, 162, 169
Ich trage deinen Namen, 167
In der Hängematte, 166, 169, 170
Kyrie, 48, 164, 169
*Lamentatiun dal pulin, dall'ochetta e dal
    pulaster*, 66, 164
Langwieser Lied, Das, 66, 164
Lass mich Gitarre sein, 167
Lied der Flösser, 166
Matg, 79, 165, 169, 170
Minnelied, 162, 164, 169
Morgentau, 48, 163, 169, 170
müden Sterne, Die, 48, 162, 170
Nächtliche Lampe, 87, 166, 169, 170

Nämlich, 168
Nichts, 167
Phoenix, 110, 167
Plainte et complainte d'un pauv' vieux chien, 85, 166, 169
Pos, o Matg, 79, 131, 165, 169, 170
Reisen, 117, 167, 169
Schmetterling, 114, 168, 170
Sehnsucht, 79, 165, 169
Sommer (In die Wolken), 167
Sonett, 165
Südliches Glockenspiel, 48, 163, 169, 170

Tod, Der, 79, 165, 169, 170
Urworte Orphisch, 167
Vier alte Spielmannsweisen, 48n, 163
Vor der Ernte, 48, 164, 169
Vorfrühling, 45, 49, 163, 169, 170
Wess' Leben so sich endet, 163
Wunsch des Liebhabers, Der, 164
Zona dal plaschair, 111, 167, 169, 170
Zwei Bündner Scherzlieder, 66, 164
Zwei Stern lüchtend hoch am Himmel, 165

General Index

Aarau, 13n, 141, 166
  Literaturhaus, 125
Adolfsen, Hans, 126
Adorno, Theodor Wiesengrund, 134, 135n
Aellig, Ruth, 118
Aellig, Simon, 118
Albrecht, Mathilde (*née* Gut) > Gut,
  Mathilde
Alphonse Leduc, 96n
Altenburger, Silvie, 144
Amadeus Verlag, 135n
Ambach, Rudolf, 149
Amir, Tom, 156
Amriswil, 135n
Amsterdam, 86
Andreae, Volkmar, 41, 129
Anouilh, Jean, 61, 137
Apollonius Rhodius, 61, 137
Aquinus, St Thomas, 72, 154
Aristophanes
  Frogs, The, 116, 146
Arlberg massif, 18
Arnold, Willy, 68n
Arosa, 14, 29, 72
Ascona, 67
Athens, 137
Atlantis Musikbuch-Verlag, 131n, 135n
Atlantis Verlag, 135n
Augustus III of Poland > Frederick
  Augustus II, Elector of Saxony
Aurora Quartet, 144
Aversa, 38, 39

Bach, Johann Sebastian, 79
Bachmann, M. E., 158
Bad Ischl, 53
Badertscher, Fränzi, 144
Bahman, Rahman, 140
Balgach, 72n
Barandun, Brigitta, 144
Barandun, Brigitte, 140
Barandun family, 158
Barandun, Roman, 90
Barandun, Ruth, 90, 91, 96, 143, 167
Barblan, Andrea, 137

Barblan, Otto, 92
  Calvenfeier, 70n
Barth, Lucas, 49
Bartók, Béla, 69
  Music for Strings, Percussion and Celesta,
    54
Basel, 23, 35, 37, 52, 53, 73, 86, 93, 103,
  113, 123–26, 128, 138, 144, 146, 148, 151,
  154–57, 160
  Gallery Maison, 44, 123, 154–57, 160
  Multenweg, 93
  Museum der Kulturen, 126, 138
  Steinenring, 123
Baselland, Canton, 123, 159
Baumann, Ursula, 144
Beck, Conrad, 131
Beethoven, Ludwig van, 41, 44, 134, 135
Bellelay (psychiatric institute), 117
Berg, Alban, 45, 87, 103
Berkeley, Ca., 135n
Berlin, 23, 67, 71, 84, 94, 131
  Wall, 114
Berlin Philharmonic Orchestra, 94
Bern, 52n, 116n, 142, 149
  City Theatre, 70n
Bernard, Emanuel, 34, 35
Beromünster, Studio Orchestra > Zurich,
  Radio Orchestra
Bethge, Hans, 157, 164
Biała Podlaska, 146
Biedermann, Hans, 72n
Bihr, Hanny, 68n
Bihr, Joseph, 68n
Binningen, 123, 125
Birmingham, 116n
Black Sea, 63n
Bleibtreu, Karl, 23
Bleidorn, Klaus, 146
Blonay, 69
Blum, Pia, 125
Blum, Robert, 131
Bodensee-Sinfonie Orchester > Lake
  Constance, Symphony Orchestra
Bodensee-Verlag, 135n
Bolliger, Albert, 147

Bologna, 56
Bongera, Giovanni, 158
Bonn, 118, 146
Boston Symphony Orchestra, 102n
Boulanger, Nadia, 96
Bove, Cilly > Keel, Cilly
Brahms, Johannes, 23, 28, 98, 99, 134
    'O, wüsst' ich doch den Weg zurück',
    Op. 63, No. 8, 98
Brancovici, Constanţa, 54–56, 161
Brandt, Jobst van, 154
Braschler, Otto, 86, 87
Breitkopf & Härtel, 110
Brill Fink, 117n
Britten, Benjamin
    Peter Grimes, 132
Brockman, Kimberley, 126
Brodard, Michel, 152
Brotbeck, Roman, 117
Brunner, Adolf, 131
Brunner, Linus, 15n
Brütsch, Tino, 154–57
Büchel, Hans Georg, 118, 146
Budapest, 38, 131
Bündner Herrschaft, 17
Bündner Jahrbuch, 90n
Bündner Monatsblatt, 40n
Bündner Oberland, 18, 23
Bündner Zeitung, 89
Burkhard, Willy, 52, 53, 55, 59, 60, 69, 70,
    131, 132
    Gesicht Jesajahs, Das, 52
    Toccata for String Orchestra, Op. 55, 52

Caduff, Gian, 45, 79, 90, 131, 162, 165
Cajöri, Christoph, 143
Calamus Trio, 88, 108, 144
Calanda (mountain), 16, 23
Calven, Battle of, 70n
Cambridge, 136
Camerata Zürich, 55n, 91, 94, 157, 158
Cappella Nova, 171
Casal Quartet, 103, 170
Cava dei Tirreni, 38
Chanfón, Carlos, 137
Cherbuliez, Antoine-Elisée, 32, 33, 41, 45,
    49, 51, 67, 69, 72n
Chiasso, 56, 88
Choir of Gonville and Caius College,
    Cambridge, 157
Chor Chantier Vocal, 156
Chumachenko, Ana, 91, 169
Chur, 13–15, 17–19, 21, 23–25, 27–29, 32,
    34, 35, 37, 38, 41, 44, 48, 49, 53, 55n, 56,
    63, 64, 70, 72, 79, 86, 88–91, 94–97, 105,
    108, 110, 122, 128, 130, 133, 136, 139–45,
    148–50, 152, 157–59, 161
    Cäcilienverein, 25
    Cathedral, 32, 56
    City Archives > Chur, Stadtarchiv
    City Theatre, 17, 128
    Collegium Musicum, 72n
    Evangelische Bläservereinigung, 72n
    Hofschule, 27
    Kammerchor, 72n, 94, 122, 152
    Konzertstudio, 151, 168
    Kornplatz, 21
    Marienheim, 37
    Obertor, 19
    Ochsenplatz, 19, 21
    Orchesterverein, 122, 139
    Singschule, 72n
    St Martin's Church, 49, 72n
    Stadtarchiv, 13n, 40, 51n
    Teachers' Training College, 48
    Volkshaus, 49
Churfirsten (mountain range), 41
Churwalden, 56
Claudius, Matthias, 79, 165
Clerici, Silvio, 158
Colchis, 63
Colognola al Colli, 88
Conrad, Ser Mattli, 153
Constance, 70
Corinth, 63, 137
Courvoisier, Walter, 52
Culot, Hubert, 103n
Custer, Laurenz, 68

Dachau, 75n
Dada, 84
Dadelsen, Anne de, 142, 144
Dadelsen, Jean-Paul de, 156
Dallapiccola, Luigi, 109
Darmstadt, 135
Daudet, Alphonse
    'Monsieur Seguin's Goat', 148
Dauthendey, Max, 45, 163
Davos, 22, 32, 59
Davos, Viola (boarding house), 22
Dedual, Eugen, 38
Demenga, Thomas, 116
Dengler, Urs, 147
Derungs, Gion Antonio, 95
Derungs, Martin, 44, 94n, 95, 122, 152, 170
Diletto Musicale (ensemble), 118
dissonanz, 122, 124, 126, 127n
Doll, Susanne, 171

Domat/Ems, 143, 144
Dora, Flavio, 153
du Toit, Cobus, 147
Düsseldorf, 87n

Ebersohn, Hannes, 148
Ehinger, Hans, 135n
Eichendorff, Joseph von, 23, 34, 44, 131,
  155, 159, 162
Eidenbenz, Michael, 122, 124, 126, 127n,
  135
Einem, Gottfried von
  Prozess, Der, 70
Elgar, Edward
  Serenade for Strings, 99
Ellis, Beverly, 144
Ems, 22
Engadine, 66, 110
Ensemble Aventure, 103, 144
Ensemble Miramis, 140
Enzensberger, Hans Magnus, 168
Erlenbach, 144
Eschenbach, Wolfram von, 163
Escher, Christof, 97, 141
Eschmann, Johann Carl, 129
Essen, 160
Euripides, 61, 137
Ex Libris (record label), 92, 157, 169

Fein, Eva, 49
Fennica Trio, 109, 122, 145, 170
Fiesole, 38
Florence, 21
Fortunatus, Venantius, 155
Frankfurt am Main, 23n
  Cäcilien-Verein, 23n
  Hindemith Institute, 71
Frederick Augustus II, Elector of Saxony,
  45n
Freiburg im Breisgau, 103
Freie Rätier, Der, 49n, 79
Frey, Adolf, 154
Frickart, Rolf, 138
Fröhlich, Theodor, 129
Fuchs, Robert, 52n
Furtwängler, Wilhelm, 75n

Gaienhofen, 73
Gartmann, Luzius, 141
Gartmann, Thomas, 102, 140
Geilinger, Max, 158
Geneva, 52n
  Conservatoire, 70n
  University, 52

Georgia, 63n
Gershwin, George
  Porgy and Bess, 71n, 132
Gilbert, Elke, 84
Gillespie, Susan H., 135n
Gindraux, Frédéric, 154–57
Giordani, Giuseppe, 116
Giovanoli, Mario, 143
Gir, Paolo, 86
Glaetzner, Burckhard, 95
Glarus, Canton, 88
Goethe, Johann Wolfgang von, 30, 45, 55,
  61, 66, 72, 152, 155, 156, 158, 161, 167
  Faust I, 34
  Faust II, 153
Gohl, Käthi, 146
Gołębiowski, Romuald, 109, 122, 123, 146
Goll, Friedrich, 32
Goms, 118
Gonzato, Guido, 56–58, 88
Gottfried Aegler (publisher), 144
Gotthard Pass, 28
Götzis, 21, 22
Graubünden, 13–17, 48, 49, 59, 63, 66, 70n,
  79, 86, 90, 92, 95, 108, 110, 118, 121
Gražinytė-Tyla, Mirga, 116n
Greif, Martin, 48, 157, 164
Grieg, Edvard, 109, 114
Griffiths, Howard, 99, 170
Grillparzer, Franz, 60, 61, 137
  Golden Fleece, The, 60
Grisons > Graubünden
Groth, Klaus, 98
Grüter, August, 23n
Grupello Verlag, 87n
Guild Music, 144, 147, 148, 152, 156, 162,
  163, 165, 166, 168–71
Günther, Johann Christian, 45, 162
Gut, Alberta, 21
Gut, Mathilde (Meinrad Schütter's
  biological grandmother), 21, 22
Gut, Sophie > Hegner, Sophie
Gysi, Fritz, 67

Hamburg, 61
Handel, George Frideric
  Agrippina, 98, 99
Handschin, Theophil, 122
Haug, Hans, 119
Häusler, Rudolf, 68
Hay, Fred C.
  *Concerto for Piano and Chamber
    Orchestra*, Op. 72, 52
Hegner, Emilie > Schütter, Emilie

Hegner, Meinrad, 21
Hegner, Sophie (Meinrad Schütter's
  'wrong' grandmother), 17, 21–27, 37
Henning, Jürgen, 68n
Herbst, Adolf, 84, 85, 87
Hermann, Fritz, 84–86, 125, 167
Hess, Hildi, 86
Hesse, Hermann, 49, 73, 75, 97, 130, 131,
  138, 157
  Narziss and Goldmund, 75
Hindemith, Paul, 53, 55, 67–73, 76, 102,
  103, 131, 132, 148
  Cardillac, 71n
  Craft of Musical Composition, 68, 69
  Mathis der Maler Symphony, 70
Hindermann (publisher), 154
Hirsau, 147
Hirsau, Church of St Aurelius, 147
Hirsau, Klosterfestspiele, 147
Hitler, Adolf, 38, 56
Hitzig, Walter, 96
Hoby, Beatrice, 153
Höltzel, Martin, 95
Howe, Eva, 68n
Huber, Hans, 52n
Huber, Klaus, 52n
Huber, Kurt, 152
Huber, Walter-Simon, 68n
Hug (music publisher), 68n, 135n
Hug, Fritz, 87
Hügli, E., 155
Humm, Rudolf Jakob, 84, 161
Hunziker, Max, 84, 85
Huonder, Stefania, 90, 93, 109, 110, 114,
  115, 122, 123, 159, 160, 167–70
Hustedt, Carsten Johannes, 109, 114, 117,
  118, 146, 147, 159, 160, 170, 171

Ilanz, 63
Imfeld, Martin, 88, 112, 144, 145
Immoos, Raphael, 171
Innsbruck, 18
International Summer Festival, 95, 141,
  143, 157
International Society for Contemporary
  Music, 124, 131, 132
Iron Curtain, 116n
ISCM > International Society for
  Contemporary Music
Isler, Dorothea, 141

Jacobi, Erwin R., 68
Janáček, Leoš, 90
Jaunet, André, 95

Jecklin, Heinrich, 89
Jeffers, Robinson, 126
Jenatsch, Jürg, 15
Jöhl, Werner, 69
Jung, Carl Gustav, 122
Juon, Lucius, 64n, 72, 94, 152, 161
Juon, Paul, 92, 109
Just, Josias, 88, 144, 170

Käch, Hugo, 68
Kaegi, Werner, 68, 73, 75, 138
Kafka, Franz, 70
Kaltenbach, Rolf, 92
Karajan, Herbert von, 94#
Karg-Elert, Sigrid, 52n
Karst, Gebhard, 79, 165
Katkus, Donatus, 118, 147, 171
Kayser, Hans, 114
Keel, Cilly, 25
Keilberth, Joseph, 71
Keller, Gottfried, 14, 16, 45, 153
Keller, Helen, 49, 91, 152, 157, 169
Kelterborn, Rudolf, 52n
Keller, Willy, 162
Kerényi, Károly, 54
Kinderhilfe (Swiss), 34
Klaus, 21
  Hotel Adler, 21
  Hotel Hecht, 21
Kleiber, Carlos, 76
Kleiber, Erich, 76
Klein-Waldegg, 23–25, 28
Kokoschka, Oskar, 28
Kramreiter, Tomás, 96–99, 103, 106, 109,
  133, 141, 150
Kramreiter, Virginia, 96
Krenek, Ernst, 58n
Kreuzlingen, Sanatorium Bellevue, 75
Kuhn, Brigitte, 152
Kükelhaus, Hermann, 159
Kurth, Beatrice, 110, 167
Küsnacht, 69, 79–81, 85, 102, 119, 122, 123,
  125, 126, 128, 142, 144
  Seehof, 105, 122, 147, 151
  Wangensbach Retirement Home, 113
Kyiv, 114, 159

Lake Constance, 17, 75n
  Symphony Orchestra, 79, 140
Lake Walen, 41
Lake Zurich, 80, 81
Lau, Heinz, 68
Lausanne
  Bibliothèque cantonale et universitaire,

44n
Lec, Stanisław Jerzy, 122, 146
Leeb, Hermann, 52
Lehmacher, Gisela, 146
Leibundgut, Michael, 109, 110, 122–24, 126, 154–57, 170
Lenzerheide, 95, 141, 143
Leon, Stephanie, 142
Leon, Suzanne, 142, 144
Leppert, Richard, 135n
Leubringen, 52n
Leuthold, Astrid, 144
Leuthold, Hansjürg, 141
Liebermann, Rolf, 67
  Penelope, 77
Limmat (river), 106
Linsi, Otto Georg, 93n, 110n, 114, 159, 169
Liszt, Franz, 21
  Au lac de Wallenstadt, 41
Lombardy, 66
Lucerne, Congress House, 147
Lupo, Bettina, 158
Lürlebad > Lürlibad
Lürlibad, 23, 24, 88
Luther, Martin, 35
Lysi, Oscar, 91, 169

Mächler, Joseph, 81
Madrid, 96
Maffli-Nissinen, Helena, 109, 123, 145, 146, 170
Mahlmann, Siegfried August, 157
Malans, 110, 167
Mannheim, 171
Maximilian I, Holy Roman Emperor, 70n
Mehlhorn, Wolfgang, 91, 169
Mehring, Walter, 84, 86, 156, 166
  Transatlantic Psalter, 84
Meier, Daniel, 68n
Meier, Irene, 68n
Meisser, Leonhard, 86
Mendrisio, 88
Mengelt, Claudia > Schütter, Claudia
Menuhin, Yehudi, 96
Merikanto, Aarre, 109
Merker, Martin, 160, 170
Mermet, Frieda, 117
Messiaen, Olivier
  Catalogue d'Oiseaux, 108
  Technique of my Musical Language, The, 96
Meyer, Conrad Ferdinand, 45, 113, 157
Meylan, Pierre, 135n
Michelangelo Buonarroti, 38

Milan, 67
Möckel, Hans, 139
Moeschinger, Albert, 131
Montalin (mountain), 16
Moreno, Christiane, 160
Mottl, Felix, 29
Mozart, Wolfgang Amadeus, 88, 117, 146, 171
  Flute Concerto in G major, к313 (285c), 117, 146, 171
  Symphony in A major, к201, 41
  Zauberflöte, Die, к620, 94
Muggler, Fritz, 68
Müller & Schade (publisher), 142, 144–47, 149–52, 154, 156, 157, 159, 160, 162
Müller, Luzius, 122, 139
Müller, Mathias, 109, 170
Müller, Pierre Walter, 84, 165
Müller, Roswitha, 126
Müller-Zürich, Paul, 72n, 131
Mumbai, 147
Mumenthaler, Max, 84, 152, 165, 166
Münch, Richard, 166
Munich, 21, 29, 52, 71, 91, 157
  Luisengymnasium, 156
Munich String Trio, 49, 169
Münster
  Post Hotel, 118
Musikszene Schweiz (recording label), 141, 157, 170
Mussolini, Benito, 54

Narbutaitė, Onutė, 116
Narbutienė, Ona, 116
Neeser, Andreas, 125, 160, 170
Nehring, Ardina, 144
Nepomuk (publisher), 93, 109, 110, 130, 141–44, 146, 147, 149–51, 160, 162–68
Neue Impulse (publisher), 160
Neue Zürcher Nachrichten, 52
Neue Zürcher Zeitung, 52, 94, 98, 99, 106
New York, 84, 116n
Niederwald, 118, 146
Nietzsche, Friedrich
  The Birth of Tragedy from the Spirit of Music, 54
Nijinsky, Vaslav, 75
Nogler, Gian, 86
Nordmann, Abélia, 156
Northwest Chamber Orchestra, 102, 140, 141
Novalis, 159
Novikoff, Sara, 90, 148, 150
Nureyev, Rudolf, 76

Obersaxen, 95, 141, 143, 157
Okazaki, Kale Lani, 152
Ollone, Max d', 52
Orselina, 67
Oswald, René, 90, 95, 99, 102, 109, 143, 144, 145
Ott, Karin, 55n, 91, 93–95, 109, 110n, 157, 158, 169

Pacelli, Eugenio > Pius XII, Pope
Paderborn, 117n
Pagani, 38
Palmer, Peter, 76, 99, 103, 110, 135
Pan (record label), 58n, 93n, 108, 141, 142, 144–46, 159, 162, 163, 165, 166, 168, 170
Paris, 21, 52n, 86, 96, 142
Pärt, Arvo, 72n
Pasztor, Vera, 39
Peer, Andri, 61, 93, 110, 111, 167
Peer, Oscar, 90
Pesch, Ada, 170
Pfitzenmeier, Günter, 95
Piachaud, René-Louis, 158
Pius XII, Pope, 54
Portmann, Thomas, 147
Prague, 55, 92
Pretoria, University, 147, 148
Previtali, Fernando, 54
Pšibilskienė, Audronė, 116

Racine, Jean-Baptiste, 54
  Bérénice, 54
Ragaz, Leonhard, 64
Ramsen, 170, 171
Ratzeburg, 114, 115, 168
Rauch, Men, 72, 154
RBM Musikproduktion (recording label), 147, 171
Rebstein, Antoine, 99, 170
Rederer, Franz, 78, 87
Reger, Max, 32n, 117
Reinhart, Hans, 73, 75, 97, 138
Reinhart, Werner, 58
Reinshagen, Victor, 71
Respighi, Ottorino
  Metamorphoseon, 102n
Reuental, Neidhart von, 164
Rheinau, 64
Rhine, 17, 19, 21, 23, 28, 64, 92
Rhône, 118
Rickenbacher, Hans-Jürg, 126
Riga, 71
Rilke, Rainer Maria, 45, 49, 131, 163
Rome, 37, 38, 52–56, 58, 59–61, 119

Orchestra of Santa Cecilia, 54
  Teatro Adriano, 54
Ronzi, Getulio de, 53
Rosbaud, Hans, 63, 77
Rostropovich, Mstislav, 116n
Rubeli, Alfred, 68n
Rüegg, Niklaus, 170
Ruhoff, Martin, 94, 161
Rünenberg, 123, 159
Russia, 63n
Ryan, Russel, 141

Sabati, Ana-Salina, 159
Sacher, Paul, 53
Sachs, Nelly, 45, 114, 159, 168, 170
Safiertal
  Restaurant Turrahus, 121
Salerno, Mario, 66, 158
Salge, Angelika, 137
Salim, Saudara, 86
Salis, Flandrina von, 110, 112, 167
Salzburg, 71n, 96
  Mozarteum, 96
San Bernardino Pass, 59–63, 88, 92
Santi, Nello, 76
Santiago de Compostela, 108
Sargans, 17–19, 21, 41, 59, 60
Satterfield, John, 96n
Sauerländer (publisher), 13n
Scaläratobel, 15, 24, 90, 151
Scartazzini, Andrea, 111, 124
Schacher, Thomas, 99n
Schaeuble, Hans, 170
Schaichet, Alexander, 43, 51, 52, 98, 106, 139
Schalk, Franz, 52n
'Schall und Rauch', 84
S-chanf, 86
Schanfigg Valley, 14
Schanzlin, Hans Peter, 135n
Scherchen, Hermann, 44, 52, 53, 63, 71n, 139
Schlaraffia (fraternity), 92, 96, 125
Schlenker, Alfred,
  Flüchtlinge, Die, 73, 75, 97, 138
Schmid, Elmar, 109, 170
Schmid, Erich, 71n, 129
Schmid, Martin, 48, 152, 156, 164, 166
Schmid, Roman, 147
Schneider, Francis, 93, 109
Schock (first name unknown. Meinrad Schütter's biological grandfather), 21
Schoeck, Othmar, 28, 44, 45, 58n, 69, 73, 75, 111, 114, 130, 131

Hesse Songs, Op. 44, 130
Notturno, Op. 47, 130
stille Leuchten, Das, Op. 60, 45
Unter Sternen, Op. 55, 45
Zwölf Eichendorff-Lieder, Op. 30, 44
Schoenberg, Arnold, 45, 61, 67, 71, 76, 114, 132
    Moses und Aron, 71, 132
Schoop, Hans, 68n
Schoor, Janandi van, 148
Schröder, Lothar, 87n
Schubert Quartet, 73, 154–57
Schuh, Willi, 52, 135n
Schumann, Robert, 28
Schütter, Claudia, 45, 49, 50, 63–65, 72, 77, 79–81, 84, 86, 87, 90, 95, 96, 105, 112, 159, 161, 162
Schütter, Emilie (Meinrad's mother), 17, 18, 21–23, 25–28, 37, 44, 77, 79, 128
Schütter, Joseph Johann ('Pepi'), 22, 25–29, 37, 77
Schütter, Joseph Johann (Meinrad's father), 17, 18, 20, 22, 25, 26, 31, 32, 64
Schweri, Ernst Jr, 79, 139, 140
Schweri, Ernst Sr, 29, 79
Seattle, 102, 140, 141
Sète, 86
Shostakovich, Dmitri, 90
Shumsky, Eric, 102, 140, 141
Sibelius, Jean, 114
Siberia, 116n
Sinus (publisher), 147
Sochi, 63n
Sordino ediziuns musicalas (publisher), 141
Sosnowska, Dorota, 109, 123, 145, 146, 170
Splügen, 50, 92
    Hôtel Bodenhaus, 93
Spörri, Eduard, 86, 165
St Christopher Chamber Orchestra, 118, 147, 171
St Gallen, 15n, 18
St Otmar's Church, 153
Stader, Maria, 35
Staiger, Emil, 67
Stalder, Hans Rudolf, 109, 170
Stalin, Joseph, 116n
Stamitz, Carl, 117, 146, 147, 171
    Flute Concerto, Op. 29, 117, 171
Stamm, Karl, 48, 131, 162, 163
Ständiger Rat für die internationale Zusammenarbeit der Komponisten, 44
Staub, Martin-Lucas, 159
Steiner, Peter Niklaus, 126, 137

Stocker, Ludwig, 86, 87, 124, 125
Stoecklin, Susanne, 148, 160
Stoecklin, Ute, 93n, 110n, 115, 123–25, 129, 137, 144–46, 148, 150, 151, 159, 160, 168–70
    Meinrad Schütter 1910-2006, 4, 9, 94n, 97n, 98n
Stoecklin, Werner, 103, 109
Stoutz, Edmond de, 96, 97, 98
Stradivarius Trio, 158
Straumann, Heinrich, 67
Strauss, Johann
    Fledermaus, Die, 80
Strauss, Richard, 28, 45
Stravinsky, Igor, 29, 53, 58n, 69–71, 132
    Rake's Progress, The, 70, 71n, 132
    Rite of Spring, The, 58
Strub, Urs Martin, 152, 153, 155, 161, 166
Stuttgart
    Conservatoire, 70n
SUISA, 135n
Sumatra, 86
Suretta Lakes, 92
Surselva, 63
Suter, Robert, 124
Swiss Composers' League, 135n
Swiss Musicians' Association, 41, 43, 44, 124, 131
Swisspan > Pan
Switzerland, 58n, 72n, 135

Tati, Jacques, 136
Teichmüller, Robert, 52
Terragni, Miriam, 160
Thelen, Albert Vigoleis, 87, 90, 152, 160, 166
Thew, Warren, 90
Ticino, 67, 118
Tonkünstlerverein > Swiss Musicians' Association
Tosti, Francesco Paolo, 21
Toth, Alfred, 15n
Tour de Peilz, La, 140
Trabzon, 63n
Treiber, Felix, 144
Treiber, Friedmann, 144
Trio Diletto musicale, 146
Tschupp, Räto, 55n, 88, 90, 91, 94, 95, 157, 158
Tsouyopoulos, Georges S., 68n
Tuapse, 63n
Turin, Radio, 66, 158
Turkey, 63n

Twelve-Tone Congress
  Milan (1949), 67
  Orselina (1948), 67

Überlingen, 75
Uglow, Timothy, 169
Ulbrich, Hans Martin, 144
Ungaretti, Giuseppe, 159
University of California Press, 135n
Uranus (record label), 93, 110, 162–69
Utrecht
  Institute for Sonology, 73n
  University, 73

Vaduz, 53
Vainio, Jarmo, 92, 109, 123, 145, 146, 159,
  170
Valais, 14, 118
Valangin, Aline, 53n
Vandevalle, Anne Christine, 147
Vashegyi, Ernö, 39
Vatican, 52
  St Peter's, 56
Venice, 53, 70
Veraguth, Manfred, 40
Verona, 88
Vézelay
  Cathedral, 108
Vienna, 18, 21, 22, 41, 52n, 87, 96, 130, 132
  State Opera, 94
Vilnius, 114, 116, 118, 146, 147, 171
  Conservatoire, 116n
  Palais Mickiewicz, 116
Vilters, 17, 21
Vogel, Wladimir, 67
Vogler, Carl, 41, 43, 44, 131
Volkart (company in Winterthur), 73
Volkart, Mario, Dance School, 72, 139
Vorarlberg, 21

Wagner, Richard, 44, 61, 128
  Flying Dutchman, The, 119
  Parsifal, 128
Währing, Nandor, 34, 35, 37–39, 44, 56, 72,
  154, 157, 162, 164
Waldegg > Klein-Waldegg
Waldmann, Eric, 167, 168
Walser, Robert, 45, 117, 160, 167
Walther von der Vogelweide, 21, 163
Walton, Chris, 140
Wangs, 17
Webber, Geoffrey, 157
Weber, Hans, 53n, 164
Weber, Karl, 81, 83, 159

Webern, Anton, 58n, 132
Weimar Republic, 84
Weisbrod, Annette, 95, 143
Weismann, Wilhelm, 165
Weltwoche, Die, 53
Wenger, Lisa, 72, 138
Wettingen, Gemeindebibliothek, 160
Widor, Charles-Marie, 52n
Wiesmann-Hunger, Barbara, 49, 158, 163,
  164
Wijnkoop, Alexander, 142
Willimann, Joseph, 131n
Winterthur, 52, 58, 73, 79, 135n, 139
  City Orchestra, 52, 79, 139
Witikon, Kirchgemeinde-Orchester, 140
Wolfbach-Verlag, 170
Wollheim, Heinrich, 75
Wyttenbach, Janka, 93n, 110n, 169

Yale University, 67

Zäch, Alfred, 49, 72, 139, 149
Zimmermann, Martin, 88, 144
Zinsli, Philipp, 33, 88–90, 95, 108, 112, 130,
  135, 158
Zinsli, Verena, 86–91, 104, 130n
Zizers, 30
Zizers, Johannes-Stift, 30
Zollikon, 120
  Catholic Church, 80, 81, 119
Zschokke, Heinrich, 13
Zug, Canton, 79
Zünd, Samuel, 154–57
Zurich, 16, 18, 21, 32–34, 39, 41–43, 51–54,
  61, 64, 67–73, 75–77, 79–81, 84–86, 89,
  92, 94, 96, 97, 99, 106, 108, 110, 113, 119,
  124–26, 130–32, 135n, 136, 139, 141, 143,
  149, 150, 154–57, 161, 169, 170
  Chamber Orchestra, 51, 52, 96, 97, 99,
    139, 141, 170
  City Theatre > Opera House
  Conservatoire, 32, 33, 41–44, 52, 53, 69,
    96, 131
  Conti Circle, 84, 86
  Conti Restaurant, 84, 85
  ETH, 69
  Fraumünster, 71
  Limmatquai, 69
  Neumarkt, 85
  Opera House, 39, 64, 65, 70–72, 75, 76,
    79, 80, 84, 129, 132
  Öpfelchammer pub, 16
  Pro Musica, 131
  Radio Orchestra, 53, 139

Radio Studio, 119, 139, 149
Tonhalle, 96
University, 32n, 67, 68
University of Music > Zurich,
   Conservatoire

Zentralbibliothek, 73n, 110, 130, 137,
   139, 149, 157
Zwingli, Huldrych, 136

9 780907 689706